Chitty Chitty BANG BANG

Flies Again

Frank Cottrell Boyce

Chitty Chitty BANG BANG

Flies Again

Illustrated by Joe Berger

MACMILLAN CHILDREN'S BOOKS

Chitty Chitty Bang Bang Flies Again
is approved by the Ian Fleming Estate

First published 2011 by Macmillan Children's Books
a division of Macmillan Publishers Limited
20 New Wharf Road, London N1 9RR
Basingstoke and Oxford
Associated companies throughout the world
www.panmacmillan.com

ISBN 978-0-330-54419-1

1 3 5 7 9 8 6 4 2

A CIP catalogue record for this book is available from
the British Library.

Printed and bound in India by Replika Press Pvt. Ltd.

*For the Curious Cousins – may they
remain forever curious*
FCB

Most cars are just cars. Four wheels. An engine. Some seats. They take you to work. Or to school. They bring you home again. But some cars – just a few – are more than cars.

Some cars are different.

Some cars are amazing.

And the Tooting family's car was absolutely definitely not one of those.

Not amazing.

Not different.

It was so undifferent and so unamazing, in fact, that on the last day of the summer term when Lucy and Jem strolled out of the school gates and into the holidays, they walked straight past it. They didn't even notice it was there until their father popped his head out of the window and shouted, 'Lucy! Jem! Jump in! I'm giving you a lift!'

'I don't need a lift,' said Lucy, who was fifteen years

old. 'I need to be alone.' Lucy always dressed completely in black, ever since last Christmas.

'Why aren't you at work?' asked Jem.

'Special occasion,' said Dad. 'I have Big News.'

'Good Big News? Or Bad Big News?' said Jem, who was a bit of a worrier.

'All Big News is tragic,' said Lucy sadly. 'Nothing good is ever news.'

'Wait and see,' said Dad. 'First we'll collect Little Harry from the childminder.'

Little Harry hated being strapped into his car seat. As he struggled to get free, Jem said, 'You have to be clipped in, in case we crash.'

'I lost my dinosaur,' said Little Harry.

'Are you going to tell us the Big Bad News now?' asked Lucy.

'It's not bad news. First we'll collect Mum from the shop.'

'You don't usually collect me from the shop,' said Mum, as she climbed into the front seat. 'Has something terrible happened?'

'Tragic news,' said Lucy.

'What tragic news?'

'Not tragic news,' said Dad. 'Big News. Excellent Big News.'

'Well, what is it?'

'I lost my dinosaur,' said Little Harry.

'Oh no,' said Mum. 'Not the lovely red remote-control one that Santa brought you?'

'Can we stop talking about the dinosaur and talk about my news, please?' said Dad.

'What news?'

'Well . . .' said Dad, '. . . I think we're going to need a takeaway to help us celebrate.'

They got the Celebration Banquet for Four with an extra portion of Chicken in Black Bean Sauce for Lucy – who liked to eat black food whenever she could. When it was all set out on the table, the lovely spicy smells curling into the air around them, Dad finally told them the excellent Big News.

'Children,' he said, 'and wife – my Excellent Big News is that –' he looked around the table, enjoying their expectant faces – 'I never have to work again! What do you think of that!?'

'Wow!' said Little Harry.

'Brilliant!' said Jem.

'That was unexpected,' said Lucy.

'How come?' said Mum.

'Because,' said Dad, 'I have been sacked! Hooray!'

'Hooray!' yelled Little Harry.

'Hooray!' re-yelled Dad.

'I'm pleased that you're pleased,' said Mum, 'but are you sure it's entirely excellent news?'

'If you have no job,' said Jem, 'doesn't that mean we'll be really poor and starve to death?'

'No,' said Dad. 'It means we'll be able to do whatever we want and go wherever we like. The word today,' he said, 'is *opportunity*.'

'I want my dinosaur back!' yelled Little Harry.

Dad explained the details. 'Since the day I left school,' he said, 'I have worked in a factory making tiny, tiny parts for really big machines. But now the company has a new contract making even tinier parts for even bigger machines. My fingers are just too big for the job. So they said they had to let me go.'

'Go where?' said Jem.

'Go anywhere we like,' said Dad.

'When you say anywhere,' said Jem, 'does that include abroad?' No one in the Tooting family had ever been abroad before.

'Anywhere,' said Dad, 'means anywhere in the world.' He smiled at Mum. 'And, dearest, you get first pick.'

4

Mum blushed a little and said, 'Well you always promised to take me to Paris.'

'Paris,' he said, 'is yours. The moment we are packed. Lucy?'

'Me?' said Lucy. 'I don't want to go anywhere. I want to spend my days in my room, now that I've finally got it the way I like it.' Lucy had got rid of all the ornaments and

dancing certificates from her room, painted the walls and her bookcase black. Dyed her duvet. And her pillowslip.

'You must want to go somewhere?'

'I suppose I wouldn't mind seeing the pyramids. I could sit in the desert looking at the Sphinx and think about dead pharaohs, with their gold and jewels, lying there in the desert night. Dead, dead, dead.'

'I can see we're going to need to plan our route,' said Dad. 'Go and get that map of the world from your bedroom wall.'

'The map of the world isn't on my bedroom wall any more,' said Lucy. 'The colours were too bright – yellow and blue and pink. Pastel colours depress me.'

'But I've had that map since I was a little boy. I won it for being punctual. It says so on the back. What have you done with it?'

'I stuck it up on Jem's wall.'

'Jem—'

'It was completely out of date. There were countries on there that were shut down years ago and new countries that weren't even mentioned. Instead of France it had something called Gaul.'

'It was supposed to be a historical map.'

'That's what I said, out of date. I put it in recycling.'

'*What?* Do you know how often I had to be punctual to win that prize?'

'Why would you want an out-of-date map when there's really good satnav in the car? A map like that could be dangerous.'

'Dangerous? How?'

'If you tried to use it you would get lost. People get lost all the time. Cities get lost, even.'

'What cities get lost?' said Lucy.

'El Dorado. Camelot. Troy. Xanadu. Atlantis. They were all big cities once and now no one knows where they are. They got lost. I bet it was because of out-of-date maps.'

'Maps go out of date,' said Dad, 'because countries change. And people can go out of date because their fingers are too big for the machines. That doesn't mean they should be put in a bin. Just because something's out of date doesn't mean it's no use.'

'Dad, I was talking about maps, not fingers,' said Jem. 'I didn't mean—'

'And it's all fine anyway,' said Mum, 'because I took the map out of recycling again. Here it is . . .' She spread it out on the table and touched the back of Dad's hand. 'I've always been very proud of your father's punctuality,' she said. 'It's one of his most attractive qualities, along with his boyish smile.' Dad smiled his boyish smile. 'Now, Jem, you said you wanted to go to El Dorado. Show your dad where it is on the map.'

'I don't know where it is on the map. That's the point. It's lost. I was making a point about how easy it is to get lost. If a big city can get lost, a small person can get lost.'

'It's somewhere around here,' said Dad, pointing to South America.

'Well then,' said Mum, 'we'll stop and ask when we get to the general area. The locals are bound to know. Little Harry, what about you?'

'Dinosaurs!' yelled Little Harry.

'We'll try our best,' said Dad. 'So . . . what have we got? Paris for Mum, Cairo for Lucy, El Dorado for Jem—'

'I really don't want to go to El Dorado,' said Jem.

'. . . and last of all, the North Pole for me.'

'That's the South Pole,' said Jem. 'You've got the map upside down. See what I mean about how easy it is to get lost?'

'Can you really drive to the North Pole in a car?' said Lucy. 'Wouldn't you be overwhelmed by blizzards and buried in avalanches and left untouched and frozen in the snow for hundreds of years, like fish fingers? Dead, dead, dead.'

'No,' said Jem. 'Because our car's got four-wheel drive and a super de-icer. And satnav. It can go anywhere in the whole world and never get stuck and never get lost.'

That's when the doorbell rang.

At the door was a nice young man in a blazer with a plastic identity card clipped to his lapel. 'Hello,' said Dad, reading the badge, 'Bernard.'

'Good evening, Mr Tooting.' Bernard smiled. 'I work for Very Small Parts For Very Big Machines.'

'Oh!' said Dad. 'So do I!'

'Not any more you don't.' Bernard smiled again.

'Oh yes, I forgot.'

'Perhaps you also forgot that this car – with its satnav, four-wheel drive and super de-icer – belongs to the company?'

'Oh,' said Dad. 'I did forget that. Yes.'

'Keys, please.' Still smiling, Bernard put his hand out and Dad gave him the car keys. Bernard drove away in the car. Mum put her hand gently on Dad's shoulder. 'Never mind,' she said.

'I've got no job.'

'We'll manage,' said Mum.

'I've got big fingers.'

'I like your fingers.'

'I've got no car,' said Dad.

'We'll walk,' said Mum.

'Not to Paris.'

'No.'

'Not to Cairo.'

'No.'

'Not to El Dorado, or the North Pole. We'll never go to any of those places. We'll never go anywhere.'

He stood and watched until the car had disappeared around the corner.

'The word today,' he said, 'is *stuck*.'

Mum went back to the supper table.

'When your father comes back,' she said, 'he may well be very unhappy.'

'Why?' said Jem.

'Because he's got no job, no car and no prospects,' said Lucy.

'I wouldn't say no prospects,' said Mum.

'He's much too old to get another job.'

'I lost my dinosaur,' said Little Harry.

But when Dad came back to the table, he said, 'Pass me a prawn cracker, Jem,' and leaned back in his chair with a big smile on his face. 'I am so glad,' he said, 'that that car has finally gone. I never wanted to travel the world. Now I'll be able to concentrate on my plans for this house.'

'You've got plans for the house?' asked Mum. 'What sort of plans?'

'The word today,' said Dad, 'is *home improvement*.'

There was a terrible, blood-curdling scream, a scream that rattled windows seven streets away.

When Lucy woke up on that first day of the summer holidays, she was confronted with her worst nightmare. While she was sleeping, someone had somehow covered her black walls with jolly blue wallpaper with daisies on it.

'My eyes!' shrieked Lucy. 'The wallpaper is blinding me!' She covered her face with her hands and, peeping out through her fingers, saw Dad up a ladder hanging a strip of the blue daisy wallpaper.

'What do you think?' he asked. 'Thought I'd brighten the place up a bit. Your room was so gloomy.'

'I like gloomy,' said Lucy. 'Gloomy is the point. I worked hard on gloomy. I painted it with three coats of gloomy paint. And what is that terrible smell?'

A little cloud of thick black smoke was curling from a hot, bubbling hole in the top of her skull-shaped reading lamp. 'My skull,' she shrieked. 'My skull is melting!' The lamp was charred and twisted and slumped to one side.

'The light seemed a bit dim so I put a more powerful

bulb in it. Maybe a bit too powerful.'

'I'm being poisoned by my own bedside lamp!'

From the next room came a cry of, 'Help! Help! Help me!'

'Oh,' said Dad. 'Sounds like Jem's awake.'

'It sounds like Jem's in mortal danger.'

'I think he's just really surprised at what I've done to his room.'

Jem had been woken up by a strange, electric whining. When he opened his eyes, a small blue object whizzed right past his face. He barely had a chance to blink when a small red object rattled past even closer. He just had time to see that the objects were car-shaped. Tiny cars were flying round his room, skimming by his face, like angry insects.

'Help!' he yelled, sliding under the duvet. 'Help!' He didn't shout anything more specific because he couldn't figure out what kind of help a person should ask for if attacked by tiny cars – presumably driven by tiny men.

The explanation was simple enough. When Dad was ten years old, he had woken up on his birthday to find that his dad had assembled an amazing Scalextric track in the bedroom he shared with his brother. It was one of the happiest memories of his life – a plastic racetrack, two racing cars – one blue and one red – and a little man with a chequered flag, all set up and ready to go. They spent the whole day racing each other round and round that track. For years afterwards they used pocket money to get extra track and the round circuit grew into a spaghetti of twists, turns, chicanes and flyovers. They grew out of it but Dad could never bear to give it away or throw it out so it had ended up in the loft. He always meant to get it down and fix it up so that Jem could play with it. Now that he'd been sacked he finally had the time to get the pieces down, make sure the wheels were oiled and the wires were snug, sneak into Jem's room and snap together a race course that whirled around the table legs, soared over his bed, swung in and out of the windowsill and filled the room with speed and the smell of hot metal.

'What do you think?' said Dad, sticking his head round the door.

'What's it for?'

'We can race against each other.'

'Haven't you heard of computers? We can race against each other on a range of platforms in any format we like. We can race as elephants, rockets, chariots – not red and blue plastic cars. And you don't have to tidy up afterwards and it's not dangerous. That's why people like to play on their computers and why they put this stuff in the dump.'

'How is this dangerous?'

'Electric wires, bits of plastic flying around the room at speed. Of course it's dangerous . . .' Just as he said that, the blue car missed the turn, shot off the end of the track, tumbled through the air and whacked Dad in the middle of his forehead. For a second it looked like he was going

to fall over. Then, 'That's
all part of the fun of it!'
He smiled and wiped the
blood away. 'The word
today is *fun*.'

Little Harry had a dream about dinosaurs. It wasn't a
nightmare. He loved dinosaurs and in the dream they were
picking him up and throwing him to each other, slapping
him into the air with their tails and bouncing him off their
horns, and all the time he was laughing and gurgling.

When he woke up, Dad was sitting on the end of his
bed.

'I know what you're going to say, Little Harry,' he said.
'You say the same thing every morning. Every morning
you say, "Play with me". Every morning I say I can't
because I'm going to work. But this morning is different.
Go on, say, "Play with me".'

'Dinosaur!' said Little Harry.

'No, like this . . . Play with me.'

'Please dinosaur.'

'Play. With. Me . . .' The moment Dad said this, there was a strange whirring from the toy box at the end of Little Harry's bed. The whirring was followed by a clicking.

'You're always asking people to play with you,' Dad explained, 'when they're too busy. So I've used some of the skills and expertise I learned in the twenty years I worked without complaint and never once being late at Very Small Parts For Very Big Machines. I have used those skills so that instead of playing with toys like other children, you will have toys that play with *you*!'

Little Harry was staring at the toy box. His eyes were growing wider and wider.

'Voice-activated,' said Dad. 'From now on, whenever you say "Play with me", your toys will just get up and play with you . . .'

Harry's eyes were now so round they looked as though they were going to fall out of his face. A dozen Playmobil men clambered out of the box and marched towards his bed, their plastic arms held out in front of them like tiny primary-colour zombies. They were followed by some wooden knights brandishing sharp little wooden lances, and a family of grinning yellow ducks that rocked themselves bit by bit across the carpet. Toy cars whizzed towards him from every dusty corner of the room.

Little Harry saw this brightly coloured army of toys coming towards him and he cried like a baby. He was a baby.

A large snake made of red and blue felt reared up from behind the washing basket and flung itself on to the bed.

A massive fuzzy blue giraffe stood up, steadied itself and began to goose-step jerkily towards him.

'They all want to play,' said Dad. 'You want to play and they want to play. It's the ideal arrangement.'

The pterodactyl mobile that hung from Little Harry's lampshade spun faster and faster until the tiny pterodactyls broke free and came buzzing round his head like Jurassic fighter planes. Desperately Little Harry tried to bat them away.

'Don't worry, they won't hurt you.' Dad smiled. 'I fitted little sensors to the front so that they don't bump into you. I'm particularly proud of those. Well, you have fun. I'm going to go and make some tea.'

Dad strolled out of the room, but when Little Harry tried to follow him the big blue-and-red snake wrapped its fluffy coils around his middle and began to squeeze. Little Harry screamed louder than ever, though his screams were muffled slightly by the massive giraffe which was now headbutting him, softly and repeatedly. He was still there being cuddled by the snake and headbutted by the giraffe when Lucy came into his room to look for a paintbrush.

'Jem! Quick!' she yelled. 'Little Harry's toys have gone nutzoid!'

They peeled the snake off Little Harry and forced the giraffe back into the corner. They locked the little wooden knights away and tied the pterodactyls down.

'What happened?' said Jem once Little Harry had been rescued from his toys.

'Isn't it obvious?' said Lucy.

'Home Improvements,' said Jem.

'Dad has got to be stopped,' said both of them.

Truly Jem and Lucy thought that as soon as Mum found out about the headbutting giraffes and melting skulls she would put an end to home improvements. But that afternoon, as she trudged up the garden path after a hard day's work at Unbeatable Motoring Bargains, a very refreshing thing happened. The front door opened all by itself and a bright little voice said, 'Do come in. The kettle is on.'

'What a lovely homecoming,' said Mum, strolling into the kitchen just as the kettle came to the boil.

'I installed an automatic self-opening on the front door,' explained Dad, 'and hooked it up to the kettle.'

'My genius.' Mum smiled.

'The word today,' said Dad, 'is *welcome home*.'

'That's two words,' said Lucy.

'Dad made a robot snake that tried to strangle Little Harry,' said Jem.

'It was a cuddly snake. It was just cuddling him,' explained Dad. 'From now on, whenever you come home, the kettle will always be boiling.'

'Also, Jem's bedroom is now a death trap,' said Lucy.

'A work in progress,' said Mum, sipping her tea. 'Be patient. Your father can't improve every aspect of our lives in one day.'

'He made my skull melt,' said Lucy.

'Teething problems,' said Mum. 'Any man who can

get a door to make a lovely cup of tea like this can do anything. Give him time.'

As far as Mum was concerned, a self-opening front door that made tea was a magnificent home improvement. The only problem was, it was magnificent for anyone who happened to be passing. When Mum came down next morning, the milkman and the paper boy were already in the kitchen guzzling tea and Krispies. The paper boy looked hard at Mum and said, 'I know you from somewhere.'

'I live here,' said Mum. 'Those are my Krispies.'

'Thanks for sharing,' said the paper boy.

There was a sudden draught of cold air as the front door opened itself and invited a passing jogger in.

'I,' said Mum, 'have to go to work.'

Off she went.

The postman, the milkman and the paper boy all left to resume their work quite soon after Mum, but the jogger was not in any hurry. He was still there when Lucy and Jem came down to breakfast. Still there when Dad came in to cook lunch. Every now and then he did stand up as if about to leave, but each time he did the front door would ask another jogger in and the joggers always seemed to know each other and have plenty to talk about. Slowly the kitchen filled up so that by four o'clock it was an impenetrable mass of joggers. If Jem or Lucy looked in, someone would push a mug at them and say, 'More tea, please,' or, 'We've run out of milk.' The children parked themselves miserably on the bottom stair, waiting for the day to end.

'I'm hungry,' said Little Harry.

'We have been excluded from our own kitchen,' said Lucy.

'I'm hungry,' said Little Harry.

'So am I, but there's nothing we can do about it just now.'

'I'm hungry,' said Little Harry.

'Yes. You've mentioned this. Why can't we just be an ordinary family like we used to be?'

'You were ordinary,' said Lucy. 'I never was.'

Outside the house someone was happily honking a car horn.

'Who's that?'

'It doesn't matter who it is,' said Lucy. 'It doesn't matter if it's Lord Voldemort and his wicked stepmother, the front door will still open and ask them in for tea.'

The front door did open and did ask them in for tea, and when it did they saw, standing in the road, a dirty blue-and-cream camper van with rusty bumpers and one window missing.

'Mummy!' yelled Little Harry. For there, behind the wheel, waving and honking the horn, was Mum.

'What,' said Jem, 'is *that*?'

They all hurried outside.

'That,' said Dad, 'is a 1966 camper van – a twenty-three-window Samba Bus – the kind enjoyed by adventurous families for over half a century now. Am I right?'

'Exactly right,' smiled Mum climbing down from the driver's seat. 'Twenty-three windows. Counted them myself. Bargain of the week at Unbeatable Motoring Bargains.'

'Half a century?' said Jem. 'Are you sure? It looks a lot older than that. It looks medieval.'

Dad peered inside. 'Look at this gorgeous old steering wheel,' he said, 'and the old-fashioned gauges. I bet the horn sounds like a choir.' He honked the horn, and the front bumper fell off and broke into pieces on the pavement.

'That kind of thing does happen with old cars,' said Dad, 'but it's nothing that can't be fixed. Look, it's got the classic split windscreen. It looks like two big eyes. When you see it from a distance it's like a big smiley face. Go on. Take a look.'

'If you look at it too hard,' said Jem, 'it will fall completely to pieces.'

Dad ignored him. 'It's got a pop-up roof compartment for extra sleeping space and a pull-out awning. Ideal for picnics on rainy days. That's the handle just over the door. All you have to do is give it a hearty tug.' He gave the handle a hearty tug. The door fell off.

'Oh,' said Mum. 'Oh dear.'

'Oh dear,' said Dad.

'I knew it,' said Mum. 'I've bought a wreck. It's just that when you talked about us all going round the world together in a car, it sounded so exciting. I thought, if we had a car . . .'

'But that's not a car,' said Jem. 'Cars have four-wheel

drive, satnav and super de-icers. This has . . .'

'Charm,' said Mum.

'Exactly,' agreed Dad, looking at it sideways. 'It has charm. And character. Also the classic split windscreen.'

'What is charming,' asked Jem, 'about a bucket of rust in the shape of a van?'

'I've been so silly,' said Mum. 'I thought that you might be able to improve it – the way you've been improving the house. I thought you might be able to fix it, but I can see now that this is beyond even your talents.'

'Well,' said Dad, walking round the van and looking at it a little bit harder, 'I'm not sure about it being *completely* beyond my talents.'

'Oh it is,' said Mum, 'completely beyond. It would take someone much cleverer than you to fix a van like this.'

'Well, you know, I am pretty clever.'

'Not that clever.'

'Let's see.' He walked round the van again, the opposite

way this time. 'You know,' he said, 'this car does need work. But a car like this is not just a heap of components. A car like this is more than the sum of its parts. Bits can fall off. You can put new bits on. The car – the heart of the car – will stay the same.'

'Cars don't actually have hearts, Dad,' said Jem.

'They do have history. A car like this, it has meant something to someone.'

'Great,' said Jem, 'so you're going to put it in a museum?'

'The word today is *give it a go*.'

'Which is four words,' said Lucy. 'Not meaning to be picky.'

Dad was already busy poking about in the engine. Mum looked at Lucy and Jem and winked. Then she chased all the joggers out of the kitchen, and Little Harry cheered as they ran into the road, as though it was the start of an Olympic event.

*

In bed that night Jem was lying awake listening to his dad still working on the engine outside when Lucy slid around the door with an armful of Little Harry's soft toys. 'He's scared that they're going to try and cuddle him to death again. You'll have to keep them in your room.'

'Can't you keep them in your room?'

'Their faces are too smiley,' she said. 'Happy faces depress me.'

'You don't think they're really going to make us go round the world in that old van, do you?' said Jem. 'I mean, even if he fixes it, it will still be an old van. No interior climate control, no airbags. It doesn't even have central locking.'

'Of course not.' Lucy was laughing. 'Who'd steal it anyway? Don't you get it? Listen, Mum is worried about Dad. He's lost his job. He's lost his car. But he hasn't lost his cleverness. He's got to find something to do with it. So he's been going round ruining my bedroom and turning Little Harry's toys against him. He's got to be stopped. You said so yourself. And that's what the camper van's for. It's a total wreck. He'll never be able to fix it really. But it'll keep him busy, keep him out of trouble, keep him happy and stop him doing his home improvements.'

'But he's working really hard on it. He's still out there now.'

'So Mum's idea is working, isn't it? You see, Jem, Dad is very clever, but Mum is cleverer.'

If Lucy had put all her thoughts into an essay and a teacher had marked this essay she would have got eight out of ten. And the marks would have broken down like this:

1. Dad is a clever man.   Correct.

2. He used to use his cleverness
   all the time at work.   Correct.

3. Now he's got no work so
   he has to find something
   else to do with his cleverness.   Correct.

4. Yesterday his cleverness made
   him destroy my bedroom and
   make dangerous toys.   Correct.

5. He had to be stopped.   Correct.

6. So Mum has found something
   for his cleverness to do.   Correct.

7. Dad will be completely happy using
   his cleverness to fix that van.   Correct.

8. That van's a real wreck.   Correct.

9. So much of a wreck that even
   he won't be able to fix it.   Incorrect.

10. We can get back to being a completely
    normal and boring family.   WRONG. Wrong,
                                             so very, very,
                                             very wrong.
                                             As wrong as
                                             a person could
                                             possibly be.

Jem was woken by the sound of tapping and hammering out in the street. Dad was already up and working on the camper van – yanking long curly wires out from somewhere under the chassis, sorting screws and cogs carefully into piles, sometimes standing back and scratching his head, sometimes pouncing on some tiny nut or bolt and holding it up for closer inspection. Glancing round, he saw Jem looking down at him from his bedroom window and gave him a big smiley thumbs-up.

He really did seem very happy.

Which made Jem feel very bad.

There was Dad – all busy and excited – working away at something everyone else thought was hopeless. He really believed the rest of his family couldn't wait for him to get that van fixed, when all they wanted was for him to stay outdoors and leave their stuff alone. When Dad looked up and waved at Jem for a second time, Jem could stand the guilt no longer. He went down to the kitchen and made Dad some tea and toast.

'Thanks,' said Dad, without looking up. 'Put it over there, will you? If you just take this . . .' He pushed a long, greasy piece of piping into Jem's hands. 'Hold it still, please, while I . . .' He picked up something that looked like a squashed baby's potty made of dirty metal and tried to fit it to the end of the pipe. 'Oh yes!' he said. 'Those two bits definitely go together.'

'Dad, are you sure this is going to work?'

'I'm going to take the whole thing apart,' said Dad, 'and then put it together again, only better. What could be simpler?'

'Shouldn't you have a manual or a diagram or something?'

'This is so old, I imagine there are no manuals left. If there are, they're probably written on papyrus or stone tablets or something. I think I just have to take this one screw at a time. It'll be hard, but it'll be worth it when it's done. This is very important to your mother.'

'Are you sure? She probably wouldn't mind, you know, if you'd rather do something else. You could hook the front door up to the toaster as well as the kettle so that it could make a whole breakfast.'

'She was so disappointed when they took the car away. I'm going to make it up to her.' Then he turned back to the van and started whistling.

His whistle was so loud and so happy that Jem couldn't bear to listen. Instead he ran into the house, jumped on to the Internet and searched and searched until he had found an intensely detailed diagram of the inner workings of a 1966 VW Samba Bus. If the van was a puzzle, here was the solution. He printed it out and gave a copy to Dad. Dad stared at it as though it was a treasure map. 'This,' he said, 'changes everything. Now we know what we've got and what we haven't got. Look. That weird thing that looks like a rubber millipede, that's the carburettor seal. I would never have guessed that. And these things like vicious paper clips, they're for the interior wiring and there should be fourteen of those and . . . there are!'

'These springs,' said Jem, 'are for the awning-release mechanism. Those little wheels go under the seats so you can move them around . . .'

Before the diagram, all the bits of metal and rubber spread out on the driveway were nothing but dirty, old junk. After the diagram, they were pieces of the biggest, most complicated jigsaw puzzle ever. The thing about jigsaw puzzles is, no matter how boring the final picture might be, if you walk past one that someone else has started, you can't help but pause to see if you can spot a missing piece. In a puzzle, every single piece is important. The rustiest, tiniest screw is brighter and more valuable than the brightest, most valuable treasure if it's the screw you're looking for. That's how it was for Jem. He couldn't help looking. When he found the right place for the right piece, he couldn't help being excited. After all, this was not any old jigsaw. They were not just making a picture of Buckingham Palace or the Alps in spring. They were building something that would make

a noise and move around and take you places.

So that's how Jem and his dad spent those first long days of summer, prowling through the piles of van components, looking for just the right parts, scrubbing them with wire wool, oiling them, comparing them, swapping them, fitting them together. Sometimes they spent half a morning discussing and scrutinizing one length of tubing. Other times they didn't say a word for hours on end. Through it all, Little Harry sat in the front seat, swinging from the steering wheel, pretending to drive, imagining the world whizzing by. When Mum left home for work, they were usually already out there. When she came home from work, they were always still out there. When the sun went down, they barely noticed but kept on going until they couldn't see a thing. Sometimes

they forgot to eat lunch. Sometimes they sat with a pile of sandwiches and spent the whole afternoon chewing and thinking. The days rolled into each other, though one or two stood out as the dates of some great victories:

29 JULY
The day they stopped the exhaust rattling

3 AUGUST
The day they got the door back on its hinges

8 AUGUST
The day they figured out how to make the roof go up and down

13 AUGUST
The day they realized that those long thin things were in fact foldaway beds

14 AUGUST
The day Dad pulled a handle and, instead of a door falling off, the awning slid beautifully and smoothly out of its compartment.

Dad and Jem and Little Harry sat down in the shade of the awning and talked for the very first time about the places they might go when the van was ready. Mum came out with tea and biscuits and said, 'That is a horrible awning.' It was tatty, with green and blue stripes. 'No one will want to sit under that. Wait there.' She went to the loft and found, hidden among the junk and souvenirs, the curtains that had hung in Lucy's bedroom before she swapped them for black blinds. They were a bright, sandy yellow with pictures of sandcastles and parasols. They made the perfect awning.

Of course, once the awning was perfect it became obvious that certain other things were far from perfect. The seats had holes in them. The bodywork was covered in dents and scratches. The tyres were encrusted with mud and oil.

They polished headlights, buffed chrome, touched up paintwork and blackened tyres. They even repaired the bumper that had fallen to pieces that first day and shone it up till it looked as good as new.

Once the outside was done, they started on the inside. There were seats that turned into beds and a table that you could make bigger or smaller. They found fresh linen cloths for the table, and flowery duvets and pillowslips for the beds, with curtains for the windows. They hung the pterodactyl mobile from the ceiling. They pillaged the loft and the cellar for reading lamps, storage boxes, shelves for books and Travel Scrabble. They made sure the little gas cooker was in working order. Outside

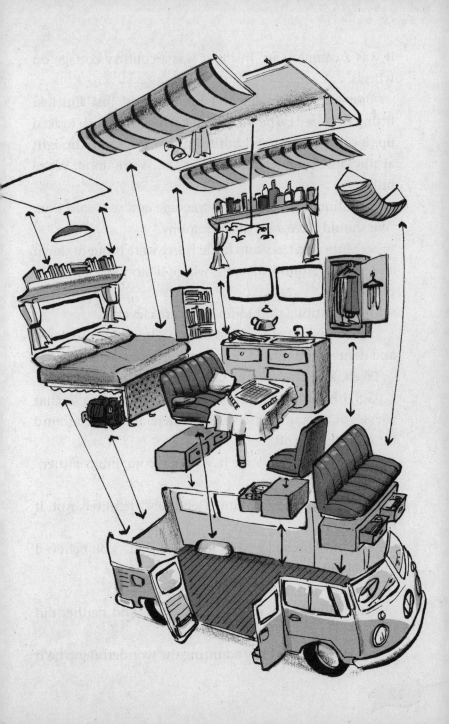

it was a camper van. Inside it was a country cottage on wheels.

One afternoon, Jem and his dad had just finished fitting thick red carpet in the back when they both looked up, looked around and both thought the same thought at the same time – namely, That's it. We're done. We're finished.

'We should get the others to come and see,' said Dad. 'We should have a bit of a ceremony.'

So Mum and Lucy and Little Harry were brought down and shown around the van, where it stood gleaming in the road.

'It's beautiful,' said Mum. 'You are clever.'

'I preferred it before,' said Lucy. 'When it was battered and dented and ruined. It was much more romantic.'

'Well, it wasn't all me,' said Dad. 'Jem helped a lot.'

'So,' hissed Lucy, glaring at Jem, 'it's all his fault that we've got to cram ourselves into there and drive around for months on end.'

'I couldn't have done it without your mum either,' said Dad.

'I didn't help!' said Mum. 'Definitely, definitely not. It was all you.'

'Yes, but you believed in me,' said Dad. 'You believed that I could do it.'

'Actually, no, I didn't,' said Mum.

'She really, really didn't,' said Lucy. 'And neither did I.'

But Dad was too busy admiring the wonderful job he'd

done to listen to them. He just thought everyone would be as happy as he was.

'So now, thanks to you,' Lucy went on, still glaring at Jem, 'we have to gather our belongings, squeeze ourselves into this old van and leave all our friends and hopes behind to wander the Earth like ghosts. Or refugees. Or some other wandery thing. Lost, lost, lost. Like a tragedy.'

'Lucy,' said Mum, 'you love tragedies.'

'Not,' said Lucy, 'when they happen to me.'

'The word today,' said Dad, 'is *ignition*.' He climbed into the driver's seat. Jem held his breath. A few weeks ago this had been a pile of junk cluttering up the pavement. Could it be that he and Dad had turned that junk into something that really worked? Dad turned the key. Jem bit his lip. Dad touched the accelerator. The engine roared. The van shook but it didn't fall apart.

'Dad,' said Jem, 'it's alive.'

Before the Tooting family packed up their things and hit the road, Dad wanted to test the van. 'Let's hope she's as good to drive as she is to look at,' he said.

Jem sat in the front passenger seat and they cruised down the high street and out of town. The van was so curvy, so perfectly finished, that just seeing it rolling down the street made people feel good.

If seeing it made you feel good, driving it made you feel amazing. Dad felt like a king in a carriage, surveying his loving subjects as they pointed from the side of the road. But while Dad was concentrating on waving and smiling, Jem was listening to the engine. In modern cars there are lights and dials and alarms that tell you everything that is happening inside. In old cars there is no such thing. In old cars you have to learn to listen to the engine, to notice any strange rattles or rumbles and try to figure out what they mean.

'Listen,' said Jem. 'Listen to that.'

'It sounds all right to me,' said Dad. 'A throaty roar, a motor that's raring to go.'

BUKKA CHIKKA BUKKA CHIKKA BUKKA CHIK

'Shh, there it is again,' said Jem.

'I can't hear anything.'

'Exactly. Every now and then you can't hear anything. Every now and then the engine misses a beat. Listen . . .' They both listened. 'I think we've got a spark-plug problem,' said Jem.

Dad shrugged. 'I'll clean them out when we get home.'

'We've already cleaned the spark plugs. More than once,' said Jem. 'They must be cracked. We'll need new ones.'

'Where will we get new spark plugs for a 1960s camper van? I ask. That is an unusual and antiquated spark plug. Surely we can manage. It seems all right to me.'

'That's because you're not really listening. An engine like this, you have to listen carefully. There is a problem with the spark plugs and we can't go thousands of miles with damaged spark plugs. I'm going to call Mum.'

'Oh dear,' said Mum, when she heard Jem's voice. 'You've broken down. Well, never mind.'

'No, we haven't. Not yet anyway. We need new spark plugs. And we thought that as you work in Unbeatable Motoring Bargains you might know where to get them.'

'My boss,' said Mum, 'Mr Unbeatable, buys all his spares from Bucklewing Scrap and Salvage. But be very careful. Bucklewing Corner is an accident black spot.'

Bucklewing Corner is first mentioned in the Domesday Book (1086), where it is called 'Bwcle Wynde Crofte' – which means 'Caution, Very Sharp Bend'. It was this sharp bend that made the Bucklewing family its fortune.

In Norman times, farmers going to market found it hard to manoeuvre their wagons around Bucklewing Corner without dropping tons of carrots and turnips and swedes into the Bucklewing field. Far more vegetables fell into that field than anyone could possibly have grown in it. Old Guillaume de Bucklewing would order his serfs to collect them all and sell them. One hundred years later, when King John was fleeing from the invading French, he was going far too fast on the approach to Bucklewing Corner and his treasure coach completely overturned, spilling gold and coins and Crown jewels all over the place. The young Bucklewing men did their very best to help him collect it all and get him on his way, but somehow they missed a few hundred gold coins and several large diamond rings. They looked after these carefully in case the king came back but he never did because he died of a surfeit of peaches. After that the Bucklewing men used the money to build Bucklewing Farm.

The Corner really began to make money in 1901 when a motorist completely misread the turn and drove his horseless carriage – a Roger-Benz of German and French manufacture – straight through the brambles, did a double backwards somersault and landed radiator down in the field. Mrs Bucklewing took very good care of the driver, who kept apologizing for ruining her hedge. He bought a dozen eggs and limped on his way, promising to come back and get the car as soon as his courage returned. It seemed that his courage never did return because the car stayed standing on its end in the middle of the field for almost a month, when it was knocked flying by a speeding Humber Voiturette, driven by a young lady who was attempting to escape from an unsuitable marriage and really had no idea how to drive at all. She hid a while in the Bucklewing barn, and when the unsuitable groom came looking for her, the Bucklewings told him she'd stolen their donkey and ridden away to the coast. A few months later the runaway bride married the youngest Bucklewing boy – Hornblower Bucklewing II. She never moved her car either. From time to time, another driver would come flying through the hedge and crash into the field. At first it was just a car or maybe two each year, but as cars became more popular, so did crashes. Soon cars were crashing through the hedge on a more or less weekly basis. It was Hornblower Bucklewing VI who decided there was no point even trying to move them. They should stop calling it a field and start thinking of it as a spontaneously occurring scrapyard. Naturally it was the fastest cars that crashed most often so the field soon filled up with expensive sports cars – Jensen Interceptors, MGs, E-Type Jaguars. People paid very good money to come and take their tyres, wing mirrors and other spare parts, or even just to come and look at them. Hornblower Bucklewing IX opened a tea room in the back of a huge wooden truck that had skidded in on the ice one Christmas. The truck had been carrying hundreds of turkeys, which the Bucklewings kept and cooked. People said the Bucklewings liked living on an accident black spot, that when the government offered to straighten the road the Bucklewings wouldn't let them, that when the local council put up a warning sign, the Bucklewings pulled it down. That's what they said.

The truth is, if the government ever really had put up a sign, it wouldn't have been long before someone crashed into it.

Dad did not crash though. He drove through the gates at just the right speed and parked next to a crumpled-up ice-cream van. A man carrying a blowtorch and wearing big gloves and a protective helmet popped out from behind it and introduced himself. 'Hornblower Bucklewing the Eleventh at your service. Have you just crashed?'

'No.'

'Coming too fast around the corner, I suppose.'

'The corner was fine.'

'If you've crashed, I'm afraid your car belongs to me. The moment your vehicle comes through the hedge, it becomes the property of Bucklewing Scrap and Salvage. There is a notice about it on the road.'

'We didn't crash,' said Dad. 'We've parked over there.'

The moment Mr Bucklewing saw the camper van, he gave a low whistle. 'That is a beauty,' he said. 'A twenty-three-window Samba Bus. I've never seen such a beauty. Where did you get her?'

'Built it,' shrugged Dad. 'Restored it. With the help of young Jeremy here.'

Jem winced. It had taken him years to trim down his big, curly, old-fashioned name to the smart, streamlined 'Jem'. Dad always Jeremyed him when he was showing off. Now this man would be Jeremying him all afternoon.

'Grand job,' said Mr Bucklewing, taking off his helmet and gloves and putting down the blowtorch. 'A very grand job. That is what you call a head-turner.'

'Do you really think so?'

'I do, and I know what I'm talking about.' He pulled a crumpled tweed hat out of his pocket and put it on his head. 'One thing I know about is beautiful cars. Why? Because foolish motorists keep driving them through my hedge, sir. Sometimes I walk around this place and look at the chrome and the leather and the paintwork and the lovely lines of these vehicles and then I think about the thick-headed drivers who wreck them and, sir, it makes me angry, sir, that's what it does. Oh so . . . angry.' On the last 'angry', he banged so hard on the wing of a nearby Porsche that his fist went straight through it and Dad had to help him get his hand out again.

'A 356 Speedster,' said the man, shaking his head sadly as he waggled his hand free. 'One of the prettiest little cars ever built, and now look at her. Abandoned and forgotten. What do you call her?'

'What?'

'Your camper van. A motor like that should have a name. It's not like it's some run-of-the-mill four-wheel drive with satnav and a super de-icer. That's a vehicle with heart, that's one you're going to need to talk to – to coax her round corners and swear at when she won't start.'

'You're right,' said Dad. 'I hadn't thought of that. Jem, what about a name for our masterpiece?'

But Jem was thinking of other things. Standing there in the scrapyard, looking around at the heaps of rusty metal and twisted fenders, he was reminded of just how much he liked things to be new and normal. Who in their right mind would want a car that you had to swear at?

'Dad,' he said, 'why don't we sell the van and use the money to buy a modern car?'

'Well, it's a thought . . .' said Dad. He looked around at the piles of battered and crumpled cars. 'I could live like this.'

'Like what?'

'You know, taking broken things – things that everyone else thinks are wrecked and finished – and making them look like new. I'd love that. Giving people hope. And cars.'

'Be my guest,' said Mr Bucklewing.

'Really?' said Jem. 'You'd give my dad a job?'

'A job?' said Mr Bucklewing. 'Who said anything about a job? Do you think I'm made of money?' He thumped the rusty Porsche again. Once again he went straight through the metal, so now his other hand was stuck in the car.

'Dad could fix the cars,' said Jem. 'You could sell them for a fortune.'

Mr Bucklewing looked at the ground. 'It doesn't really work like that around here,' he said. 'I don't like paying people.'

'Oh. I see.'

'People like to be paid money. I don't like to pay them. That leads to disagreements, and disagreements make me uncomfortable. No offence.'

'Offence?' Dad laughed. 'Of course there's no offence. I'm not against jobs, you understand, but I don't have time to take one now. We've got bigger fish to fry. We're going to travel round the world in our van here. Isn't that right, Jem? Just as soon as we can find some new spark plugs.'

'Then be my guest,' smiled Mr Bucklewing. 'Take a look around. If you can find any, they're yours. It'd be an honour to supply parts for a vehicle like that. We did have a Samba Bus crash here once back in the early seventies.

Orange, it was. Some hairy young people heading for Marrakech. Like so many others, they only got as far as Bucklewing Corner. As I recall, they crashed into a tree. Car is probably still up in the branches somewhere. Take a look.'

As he said 'Take a look' he finally managed to get his hand free of the rusted metalwork. Looking at the two jagged holes he'd punched in the Porsche, Jem thought that Mr Bucklewing probably wasn't the best person to have as your boss anyway.

Bucklewing Scrap and Salvage is a vast labyrinth of broken and rusting vehicles. Trucks lie on top of vans and cars lie on top of trucks in tottering piles of wheels and pipes and radiators. Columns of used tyres mark each corner. Herds of lorries lie about the place like dozing dinosaurs.

Jem and his dad wandered down boulevards of broken-down buses, along avenues of wrecked racers and streets of smashed-up saloons until they came to a strange patch of woodland – where oak trees and 4 x 4s seemed to be growing side by side, fenders and tyres hanging from the branches like blossom and fruit.

'There,' said Jem. The unmistakable back end of a camper van was sticking out from a tangle of brambles. The van had flowers painted on it and the brambles were covered in blossom. The boot was open, and Jem could see the spark plugs sitting in the rear-mounted engine like a row of milk bottles. All they had to do was pick them out and go.

'What's that?' said Dad, staring up into the fork of the fattest oak. 'There's something up there.'

'Leaves?' said Jem. 'Twigs? Squirrels? Come on, we've found the spark plugs. Let's take them and go.'

Dad was already pulling a ladder from the remains of an ancient fire engine. He propped this against the trunk of the oak and clambered up.

'Dad, come down.'

'Jem, come up and look at this.' Lying among the leaves like a fat sleepy cat, Dad had found an engine, but it wasn't the engine of a camper van. It was something much, much bigger. He tore the branches and leaves aside and hoisted the biggest branch over his shoulder, opening up a kind of green cave of leaves and twigs. Lying in that cave was something that looked more like a petrol-driven dragon than a car component. Honeysuckle curled in and out of its twisty complication of steel pipes and brass pistons. Moss obscured something that looked like a huge dark mouth. Squirrels and robins dodged in and out of its corners and chambers, as though the engine had simply grown here and this oak was actually a car-parts tree.

'What is it?' gasped Jem, who had finally climbed up after his dad.

'That is an engine,' said Dad. 'That is an engine and a half.'

'But how can it be an engine? It's huge. It must be from an aeroplane.'

'No. Look. There's the steering wheel.'

Dad crawled out along the branch.

'Careful, Dad. Be careful,' warned Jem.

Dad kept crawling along, snapping twigs and pulling away leaves. It really was more than just an engine. It was the whole insides of a vast, vanished car. There was the steering rack, the starter mechanism, the axles, the exhausts . . .

'Jem, come and see this . . .'

There was a twisted metal bar sticking out of the front of the engine, with a kind of handle on the end. 'Do you know what that is?' said Dad.

'No.'

'It's a hand crank. This engine must be seriously old. Instead of putting a key in the ignition, you grab hold of this and you crank it like so until the engine gets going . . .'

'Dad, don't! What if it . . .'

But it already had. As Dad turned the crank the engine spluttered, then coughed and finally roared.

'Dad! Look what you've done!'

Dad let go of the crank, but it carried on spinning, faster and faster like a propeller.

'Listen to that!' yelled Dad. 'That is a beautiful sound. That is music.'

It sounded more like an earthquake. It also felt like one. The branches of the tree shook. Squirrels scattered. Birds fled. A storm of leaves and acorns whirled around Jem's head. 'Stop! Dad! Turn it off!'

'Here's the pedal. I'm going to rev it . . .'

The engine roared louder than ever. Branches snapped. Under Jem's feet the ladder whipped left and right. 'Please, Dad! Stop!' Branches splintered. There was a terrible noise, a noise like a massive old engine falling out of a tree on to a dilapidated fire engine. And the cause of that noise? A twelve-cylinder possibly aeroplane engine falling out of a tree on to the roof of a dilapidated fire engine and squashing it like an old concertina.

'Dad!' shrieked Jem. *Dad*? Are you dead?'

'Not dead,' Dad called, 'but very, very excited.'

It wasn't long before Mr Bucklewing came along to see what the noise was. He walked around the engine, stroking his chin. 'Now that,' he said, 'is what I call a beast. A Beast! Think of the power, the strength of an engine like that, and now what is it? Just an over-complicated squirrel nest. A car like that,' he sniffed, 'should be running free, out on the road, guzzling petrol, pouring out smoke. But look at it, lying there. What a waste.' He took his hat off and clasped it to his chest as a sign of respect. 'Why, why, why? All because some thick-headed motorist drove too fast into the corner, that's why.' He pulled back his foot as if to kick the engine with his steel-capped boot.

'No!' said Dad. 'Stop! Just because something has been cast aside, abandoned, thrown on the scrap heap, does that mean it's no use? What if . . .' Mr Bucklewing's boot came nearly but not all the way down again. He was keeping a kick in reserve just in case. '. . . What if we saved this engine? What if we gave it a new life? What if we took this beautiful, neglected old engine and used it in our camper van?'

'*What*?' shrieked Jem. 'No, no, no, no. This engine's bigger than the van!'

'Well, just looking at it –' Mr Bucklewing bent down for a closer look – 'the engine in the camper van is usually fitted sideways in the rear, but what if you lifted up the whole chassis and slipped the engine underneath? What if you just made the van a bit taller so the engine could lie along the bottom? I could help you.'

'No,' said Jem. 'Every kind of car has its own kind of engine, and this is not the kind of engine for our kind of car.'

'The word today,' said Dad, 'is *customize*.'

It occurred to Jem that no one ever asked *him* what the word of the day was.

'This is a great opportunity,' smiled Dad, 'to give our van a new engine. This beautiful, redundant engine a new body.'

'This is a great opportunity,' agreed Mr Bucklewing, 'for you to make me happy –' he stared hard at Jem – 'or sad.' He stared harder at Jem. Jem decided it was probably best to say nothing.

Jem was right, by the way, about the right kind of engine for the right kind of car. The twenty-three-window Samba Bus normally has a flat-four engine. This means it's got four little pistons in facing pairs. They go in and out at the same time, so when it's working it looks as though they're playing pat-a-cake.

The engine that Dad had found had twelve big pistons in a line, worked by a mighty crankshaft. When it's working it doesn't look like a game of pat-a-cake. It looks like a battalion of furious robots punching each other to death.

The flat-four engine has a capacity of 1.5 litres.

The engine that Dad found had a capacity of TWENTY-THREE litres.

The flat-four engine was built to power a camper van.

This engine was built to power a fighter plane.

Putting an engine like that into a camper van was like putting the heart of a Tyrannosaurus rex into a hamster. Dad did it anyway. In spite of all that Jem could say. And Mr Bucklewing helped him. He used his own crane to help lift the chassis and his blowtorch to weld everything into place. The chassis fitted over the engine surprisingly well, except for the two huge exhaust pipes sticking out of the back and the massive radiator at the front.

'That exhaust . . .' Mr Bucklewing sniffed in admiration. 'It looks as though it was always meant to be there.'

'It looks,' said Jem, 'like a shark's tail on the back of a duck.'

'The radiator, oh, the radiator . . .' sighed Mr Bucklewing.

'Like a shark's jaws in a kitten's face.'

'No keys,' said Dad. 'I'm always losing my car keys. But this –' he held up the hand crank – 'is far more practical. It's going to be a lot harder to lose this. Jem, you can be in charge of it.' He handed Jem the long twisted metal rod.

'Thanks,' said Jem.

'No problem. Wait till you see . . . this . . .' He opened the bonnet and showed Jem a tiny metal plaque screwed to the top of the carburettor. 'I didn't notice it at first because it was covered in oil. But when I wiped the carburettor, there it was. See . . .' The little plaque had just one word on it. Zborowski. 'This engine has got a name. And it's the same name as our street. Coincidence? I don't think so.'

In fact Zborowski wasn't the name of the engine at all. It was the name of the man who had owned the engine – Count Louis Zborowski. He had bought the engine from

an aeroplane company (Jem was right about that) in 1921 and built a car around it, a really, really fast car. One day the count was out driving dangerously fast, when up ahead he saw a little girl run out into the road with her toy pram. The count slammed on the brakes and shot off the road into a field. The skid marks he made were so deep and straight that the council decided it would be cheaper to turn them into a road than to try to get rid of them. They called that road Zborowski Terrace. They even put a helpful diagram under the name on the road sign so that people would know how to pronouce it: ZB-OR-OV-SKI.

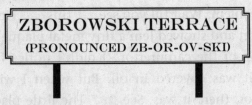

ZBOROWSKI TERRACE
(PRONOUNCED ZB-OR-OV-SKI)

'Zborowski engine,' said Dad, 'Zborowski Terrace. It's a sign. We are meant to have this engine.'

'The thing about signs, Dad,' said Jem, 'is that people misread them. That's how car crashes happen.'

'I'll take extra care when I'm driving.'

'Dad, this engine doesn't want to drive the Tooting family off to France. It wants to go screaming around racetracks and setting land-speed records.'

'This engine doesn't want to do anything,' said Dad, 'because it's just an engine. It's the Tooting family that wants to do things. The engine will do as it's told.'

How wrong can a dad be?

When Dad crank-started the camper van, Mr Bucklewing stood back and said, 'At least you won't have to think of a name now. It's called Rory, isn't it? Because it roars so loud.'

'No,' said Jem. 'Rory is a boy's name, and this is a girl.'

'A girl?' said Dad. 'It's not a girl. It's a van. Honestly! What do they teach in biology these days?'

'It's called Rory,' growled Mr Bucklewing, clenching his fist. 'Say hello to Rory.'

'Hi, Rory. OW!' said Jem.

'Ow?'

'That hurt. Look . . .' Jem had stepped on some kind of ornament that was sticking up out of the mud. It was a little silver plane, with two sets of wings, an open cockpit and a big propeller. Mr Bucklewing picked it up and, rubbing the mud off, blew on it. The propeller went round. 'Lovely,' he said. 'They don't make planes like that any more.'

'That's because planes like that were cold and noisy and dangerous. You had to fly them yourself,' said Jem.

'Mr Tooting,' said Mr Bucklewing, 'your son has no soul.'

'Oh, I wouldn't say that . . .'

'Here. Keep it.' He thrust the little silver plane at Jem. 'One day you will come to appreciate the romance, the glamour, the fineness of things that have outlived their moment.'

'Right. Well. Thanks a lot.'

When Dad and Jem pulled up outside the little house on Zborowski Terrace, Mum came out to greet them. 'Those spark plugs have made quite a difference,' she said. 'The van seems a lot louder. Also bigger. Even the exhausts seem to have grown.'

Jem wanted to tell her all that had happened, but Dad just raised his hand and said, 'Tooting family, we are ready to go. The word today is *adventure*.'

'*What*?' said Lucy when she heard. '*Now*? I have to leave all my friends and the places and people I love right *now*? I will be one of the homeless. Which I wouldn't normally mind. But in this case I'm not sure I can cope with the colours. The bodywork, the paintwork, the curtains. They're all bright, too bright.'

'I've thought of that and I bought you this.' Dad smiled, producing from behind his back a little pot of black paint and a paintbrush. 'Now wherever we go, wherever we stay, you'll be able to make it look as gloomy as you like with just a lick of paint.'

'Oh,' said Lucy. 'Thanks.'

She climbed into the van.

Really, what else could she have done?

Little Harry was strapped into his car seat. Jem spread Dad's map out on his knees. The Tooting family was ready to go. 'Fasten your seat belts,' said Dad, 'and get ready for the ride of your life.'

'Dad,' sighed Lucy, 'it's a camper van, not a jumbo jet.'

'You're right, you're right,' said Dad. 'After all, Rory's

just an old camper van. Let's not get overexcited.' Then he winked at Jem.

Jem jumped out of the van with the crank handle in his hand.

'Where's Jem going?' said Lucy. 'What's he doing?'

Jem was turning the handle, which was hard work and completely embarrassing. Who'd ever heard of a camper van that you had to wind up like a clockwork toy? What if anyone saw him? Then the engine coughed. The crank seemed to snatch itself out of his hands. He had to admit it was a good feeling, when it all suddenly came to life like that. Like the feeling when you get a bonfire to light. The engine growled, then it bellowed. By the time Jem climbed back inside the van the seats were throbbing and shaking as though they were trying to break free.

'Earthquake!' gasped Mum. 'Stay calm, children.'

'That's no earthquake.' Dad smiled as Jem got back on board. 'That is our engine.'

It was only a little blue-and-cream camper van, but it sounded like an unexpected invasion of tanks as it turned on to the high street. People looked up into the sky, expecting to see helicopters or spaceships.

'Listen to that throaty roar!' yelled Dad.

'Throaty roar?' said Mum. 'It's more like a dying man's cough.' She was right – if you listened carefully the engine made a sound like two sneezes and a cough.

'Sneezy Sneezy Cough Cough,' yelled Harry.

'This isn't a mode of transport,' said Lucy. 'This is a viral infection on wheels.'

'Sneezy?' said Dad. 'Now that's a good name. Maybe we'll call him Sneezy.'

'Does anyone else feel that their bones are turning into powder?' said Mum. 'Is that supposed to happen?'

'At the traffic lights,' said Jem, 'take the left-hand lane.'

'What?' yelled Dad. 'You'll have to shout!'

'LEFT-HAND LANE!' yelled Jem.

'OK.'

There were two lanes at the lights. Left was for straight ahead and the motorway, and right was for turning right. There was already one car waiting in the left-hand lane.

'Slow down, Dad, you're going to bump that . . .'

Dad didn't slow down. Instead the van picked up speed, then at the last moment swerved dangerously into the right-hand lane and screeched to a halt alongside the other car.

'What are you doing?' shouted Mum.

'It wasn't me! Slow down, Sneezy, you stupid thing!'

'You mean, you're not in control of this vehicle?'

'No, no. It was me. I just changed my mind at the last minute,' Dad lied. 'I thought it would be nice to go right, that's all.'

'It's a good job you didn't hit that car,' said Jem. 'It would have cost a fortune. Look.'

The car next to them was a sports car – low and red and gleaming, with thick black tyres and the top down. The driver was a young man in sunglasses. While everyone was staring at his car, he didn't even glance at the camper van. Until suddenly the engines revved.

'What on earth are you doing?' said Mum.

'The engine has a tendency to race a little,' said Dad. 'It's part of the design.'

'Hmm,' said Jem, listening carefully, 'it feels as though it's misfiring.'

'It feels like a mad dog pulling at its leash, and I'm holding the other end of the leash,' said Dad. 'Will you slow down, Sneezy.'

The engine revved again, so loud this time that the young man's sunglasses fell right off. He stared at Jem.

'He thinks you want to race him,' said Jem. 'I'd better explain.' He wound down the window. 'Sorry about the noise. I think it's a problem with the camshaft. We need to fiddle with the timing. The engine hasn't really bedded in . . .'

Suddenly the lights had changed. The camper van leaped forward, like an arrow from a bow. It was so fast that they were all thrown back into their seats. It did not turn right. It barrelled onwards, bouncing in front of the sports car and blocking its way. The back end of the van

wiggled from side to side, as if to say, 'Ha ha, I won.'

'I think,' said Lucy, 'that you are behaving in a very immature way. And I'd like you to stop.'

'I'd like to stop too,' yelled Dad, 'only Sneezy seems to disagree.'

'Please stop calling it Sneezy,' said Mum. 'I really don't want to be killed by something called Sneezy.'

By now they were on the ring road. The sports car slid into the fast lane and accelerated until it was alongside the van. The young man shook his fist at them. The van slowed down a little, allowing the sports car to speed by.

'Thank goodness that's over,' said Mum.

Except it wasn't over. No sooner had the sports car gone past them than the van lurched across into the outside lane and went thundering after it.

'Race!' shouted Little Harry.

The fields and trees were just a green blur. The cars in the middle lane flicked by as if they were standing still. The sports car look as if it was reversing towards them. In seconds they were bumper to bumper. The van's headlights flashed. Its horn blew.

'Dad!'

'Honestly, it's not me.'

'I think,' said Jem, 'that this is not just a problem with the camshaft.'

'I think this van is possessed!' Mum screamed.

'This is actually more interesting than I expected,' said Lucy.

The Zborowski engine had been designed for racing, for breaking records, but for nearly a hundred years it had been stuck up a tree with no wheels, no petrol, no purpose. Now that it was back on the road it seemed to want to make up for lost time. The Tooting family closed its eyes and screamed as the van hurled them into bends and swung them in and out of traffic. Only Little Harry kept his eyes open. He giggled and waved and shouted, 'Me drive! Me drive!' He had spent the last few weeks playing with the steering wheel while the van was parked safely outside the house. He couldn't see why he wasn't allowed to do the same now that it was hurtling crazily through queues and congestion. The little blue camper van dodged and skidded and fishtailed while all around other drivers honked their horns in anger and blinked their eyes in consternation, until finally it screamed on to the motorway.

'It was terrifying when the speed limit was forty,' said

Mum. 'What's going to happen now that it's seventy?'

The moment they joined the motorway, however, the camper van slowed down.

And down.

And down.

'Now what are you playing at, you insane internal combustion engine?' said Dad, as the lorry behind him menaced his bumper. 'We're almost stopped. What's wrong with you?'

'Nothing's wrong,' said Mum. 'Dead slow is my favourite speed.'

Jem listened carefully to the engine. It sounded as though all the power was draining from it. Yet the tank was full of petrol and the parts were moving smoothly. Nothing was stuck. Nothing was rusty. 'It sounds . . . tired. Or sad,' he said.

'*Tired*?' said Dad. 'Sneezy doesn't get tired. He's a man of steel.'

'Van of steel,' said Jem.

'In fact,' said Lucy, 'there is such a thing as metal fatigue. Maybe it's fatigued.'

'We'll have to come off at the next exit,' said Jem, 'and take a proper look.'

The camper van crawled along the slow lane to the next exit. Even with his foot flat on the accelerator Dad could only make it chug slowly up the slip road. 'There's a lay-by just a few yards along here. We'll pull in there and see what's wrong.'

They didn't pull in. As soon as they were clear of the

motorway, the van picked up speed again. Dad tried to turn into the lay-by, but the wheel just twitched out of his hands and the camper van plunged back into the traffic, following the open road round a great curve, into the hills.

'I thought you were stopping?' shouted Mum.

'I . . . errm . . . the engine trouble seems to have cleared up,' said Dad, trying to sound in control.

'The engine sounds just the same as before,' said Jem, 'only faster.'

They were bowling along the A-road now as it dipped and climbed through the rolling downs. Sheep looked up as they rumbled by.

'I know this sounds a bit strange,' said Jem, 'but I get the feeling the van just prefers this old-fashioned kind of road.'

'Sneezy does not have any preferences about what road it goes on. Sneezy is a machine. I am the driver of Sneezy,' insisted Dad. 'I decide which way Sneezy goes.'

'OK,' said Jem. 'Well, if you go right at the traffic lights, that brings us back to the motorway.'

'Maybe we'll do that then.'

The closer they got to the lights, the faster the van went.

'Dad, the lights are on red . . .' said Jem. 'You're not in the right-hand lane.'

'No,' said Dad, 'not yet. Plenty of time.' He was tugging at the steering wheel and pounding on the brakes but the van stuck to the left lane and went faster and faster.

Thankfully the lights changed to green as they streaked through, hugging the curves of the road as it swerved up and down and around the Downs, and threaded through the hedgerows and skipped over streams.

'The word today,' said Dad, 'is *spontaneity*. After all, we're in no hurry. Let's just see where the road takes us.'

'We really want it to take us to Paris,' said Mum.

'Puddles! Puddles!' Little Harry yelled, pointing at the wide blue English Channel. The sun was dropping down behind them and its rays rolled across the waters like a vast golden duvet as they pootled along the cliff-top roads. Sometimes a rabbit would run out in front of them. Once they saw a deer. At a gap in the hedge, the van slowed down and turned on to a gravel path.

'Now what are you playing at?' hissed Dad.

The van didn't answer, but Mum demanded to know where they were going.

'I thought we'd just take a breather,' said Dad, still trying to create the impression that he was in charge of the van and not the other way round. The path led across a field and through a gate, and when they passed through the gate all the Tootings gasped and smiled. For the path was lined on both sides by camper vans! Dozens and dozens of them. Battered ones, gleaming ones, vans painted in wild and crazy psychedelic colours with surfboards strapped to the roof, vans with lace curtains and pot plants in the window, vans that looked as though they had just crossed the Gobi Desert, vans that looked as if they had rolled off the production line yesterday. As the Tooting van passed by, the other drivers flashed their lights and parped their horns, greeting them in Camper-Van-ese.

At the end of the line, Dad pulled up on to some grass, but before he had time to turn off the engine, a woman with a clipboard came running up shouting, 'No, no, no, not there. You can't park there.' She was wearing a high-visibility jacket and a baseball hat shaped like a camper van.

Dad wound down the window and asked if there was a problem.

'Yes, there's a problem. You need to park in your correct category. What category are you?'

'Well . . . we're the Tooting family and we're going on holiday.'

'To Paris,' said Mum.

'And Cairo,' said Lucy.

'And dinosaurs!' yelled Little Harry.

'Yes, I'm afraid those are not proper categories. Over there, for instance, we have Classic Campers, then there's Customized Campers and Camping Crazy and what are you? You seem to have a beautifully restored 1966 Samba chassis: popular with adventurous families for over half a century, beloved by all because the split windscreen makes it look like a face.'

'Absolutely correct,' said Dad.

'Yes, I know,' said the woman, 'but that rather beautiful

bodywork is resting on what seems to be a 1920s twelve-cylinder twenty-three-litre aero engine.'

'A hundred per cent correct again.' Dad smiled.

'I know that,' said the woman. 'What I don't know is your category. You must have a category or you can't park. I can't have you messing up the lines, d'you see? Classic body. Racing engine. You're a contradiction, that's what you are.'

'Couldn't that be our category then?' suggested Mum. 'Couldn't we be in the contradiction category?'

'You can't just go around making categories up. Where would the world be if people just went around making categories up?'

'Well . . . we'd have a lot more categories.'

'Good heavens . . . what's that sticking out of the front? Is that a hand crank? A camper van with a hand-cranked engine? A *wind-up* camper van? You are not a contradiction, you are a mess.'

'Please stop calling poor Sneezy a mess,' said Dad.

'Please stop calling the van Sneezy,' said Mum, stepping out to stretch her legs. 'I've been thinking, it's a camper van and it's quite . . . unpredictable. What about Scamper?'

'That sounds like a puppy,' said Lucy.

'Yes.'

'I hate puppies.'

Jem realized then that both his parents were rubbish at thinking up names. Which presumably was why they had decided to call him Jeremy.

*

The field sloped down towards the edge of a big white cliff. Over to the left, Jem could see the port of Dover. Huge ferry boats were going back and forth across the water. They shone red when the rays of the setting sun touched them, and great plumes of smoke rose from their funnels. Looking at them, Jem felt suddenly excited. They really were going to go on a boat. Boats went over the sea to . . . everywhere. Anywhere at all. Paris, Cairo, maybe even to Lost Cities. Just because they were lost, didn't mean they'd vanished completely. They must be somewhere. Maybe he could find them. Somewhere behind him, his dad and the lady with the clipboard were still arguing about where to park the camper van but Jem's mind was already floating out across the sea, imagining jungles and deserts and pyramids. So it was a bit of a surprise when the camper van trundled slowly past him towards the edge of the cliff.

Jem looked back over his shoulder. Dad and the lady were still talking. Mum and Lucy were further along the cliff. None of them had noticed that the van was rolling away. 'Dad! Mum!' shouted Jem, then he took off after the van. It was picking up speed now but the engine wasn't running. Dad must have forgotten to put the handbrake on. Jem was sprinting, but the van rolled faster and faster. If he could just catch up, he might be able to stop it.

He could hear shouting behind him now. Mum and Dad were running after the van too. The van wobbled. Oh. The field was going uphill for a while. Thank heavens. It was slowing down. Jem was gaining on it. And gaining. He got alongside. He yanked open the door, but he couldn't reach the handbrake!

Little Harry was in the way.

Jem's baby brother was sitting in the driving seat with a smile on his face and his hands on the steering wheel, saying, 'Me driving! Me driving!' as he raced towards his doom.

'Little Harry! Jump! Jump, Little Harry!' yelled Jem, desperately trying to grab his little brother.

'Me driving! Me driving!' said Little Harry.

Jem clutched at the seat belt and tried to use it to clamber inside the cab. But the van was rolling downhill again now. Jem tried to keep up, but he wasn't running any more. He was being dragged along.

Then the van hit a bump.

Jem bounced into the air and tumbled head over heels. He leaped up, but the van was already rolling away, moving faster and faster. Dad tore past him, then Mum. Jem could still just about hear Little Harry giggling, 'Me driving! Me driving!'

And then the van was gone.

It was there.

And then not there.

The van was gone.

And so was Little Harry.

Where the little boy had been, now there was just blue sky.

*

Mum and Dad stood on the edge of the cliff looking into the blue.

Seagulls were screaming all around their heads.

'Harrrrrryyyyyyyyy!' yelled Dad.

'Nooooooo!' howled Mum.

Jem didn't scream or yell. He just stared. His brother was gone. How could the sun still be shining, the ferries still sailing, the seagulls still flying and his brother be gone?

How could the world keep going as though nothing had happened?

He knew it was too late to do anything, but he ran to the edge of the cliff. He had to look.

It seemed his mother and father didn't feel the same way.

They were running in the opposite direction. Away from the cliff. Towards him.

'Jem,' they yelled, 'get down!'

'What?'

Mum and Dad threw themselves flat on their faces and covered their heads with their hands.

Then Jem looked up and saw why.

He saw the last thing he was expecting.

It burst into view from just below the edge of the cliff, roaring like a furious bull before it rushed upwards into the sky.

It was the Tooting family camper van.

It looked exactly the same as it did when it plunged from the cliff. Except for one important detail: it had sprouted an enormous pair of racing-green-and-chrome wings. And now it was soaring high above the field. It banked. It turned. Its split windscreen eyes flashed in the sunlight and the van began to drop towards the field, its wheels spinning, its big gleaming wings rocking from side to side as it tried to steady itself, the hand crank spinning like a propeller. It was coming in to land. It was heading straight for Jem.

Jem hurled himself to the ground just in time. The smell of petrol and burning rubber whirled around his head. He could even hear the faint voice of Little Harry still happily shouting, 'Me driving! Me driving!'

There was a shower of tiny stones as the van crunched on to the gravel path. Sods of grass and bits of soil flew up into the air as it bounced to a stop. Mum and Dad ran up, pulling open the door, grabbing Little Harry and almost suffocating him with hugs and kisses and happiness.

'Oh no, no, no, no, no. Not there. You definitely can't park there.' It was the lady with the clipboard again. 'You've got wings. Wings! It's one thing adding fancy wheels or extra headlights. But wings? *Wings*!'

'Yes,' said Dad. 'When we fitted the engine we did wonder why that metal frame was so heavy. The wings must have been folded up inside. They seem to be some kind of added emergency feature.'

'Wings is going much too far. Your vehicle is no longer a camper van at all. This is an aeroplane.'

'Me flying!' yelled Little Harry.

'Aeroplanes are not allowed in the Camper Van Club. The Camper Van Club is camper vans only.'

By now the owners of all the other camper vans had gathered round. They clapped. They cheered. They took photographs.

'Please stop applauding,' shouted the woman with the clipboard. 'This vehicle is a disgrace to the camper-van community. The poor thing doesn't know if it's a van or a plane.'

But they all carried on applauding, and Dad saluted and bowed and waved and climbed into the driver's seat. Then jumped out of it again. Mum was already sitting there.

'What's going on?' he said.

'On the way here,' said Mum, 'you jumped lights, swerved all over the road, *failed to engage the handbrake*. Do you really think for one moment that I am going to let you drive ever again? Plus you thought the van was a him. You kept calling it "he".'

'It is not a him or a her. It's a van.'

'It's a girl. Of course it's a girl. Look how colour-coordinated the wings are. And the way she fell off the cliff and then came back again – so stylish, like Audrey Hepburn. She's definitely a girl. Quite a girl. Children! Climb in and fasten your seat belts. Mummy's the driver now.'

Mum started the engine and tried to drive back up the gravel pathway while the members of the Camper Van Club cheered them off. She didn't mean to take off and fly again. She just completely forgot that the wings were still extended. The faster she drove, the more they filled with air. At first this seemed to slow the van down, but suddenly there was a bump and it bounced and never landed back on the ground. One moment people were waving at them through the window, then they had all dropped out of sight, as though the ground had shrunk. Soon their faces were just little dots looking up as the Tooting family climbed higher and higher.

'Me drive!' shouted Little Harry, struggling as Dad fastened him into his car seat.

'No, your mother drive now,' said Dad in his sulky voice. 'Mummy's the driver.'

'She's not the driver,' said Lucy. 'She's the pilot.'

Dad looked out of the window and saw for the first time where they were. The cliffs of Dover were just a frilly white collar at the edge of the sea. The soft green fields were far behind them.

'Julie? Julie!' yelled Dad. 'We're in the air. We're flying in the air! We're not on the ground. We're not even over the ground. Julie! You've taken a wrong turn. A very very very wrong turn.'

'Oh, Tom,' said Mum calmly, 'do calm down.'

'I am calm. Completely calm. I am completely and utterly calm. I am completely . . . how are we going to get down? Have you thought about that? We're up in the air! How are we going to get down? We don't have parachutes. We don't have emergency exits. We have to get down. How are we going to get down? Please get us down now.'

'Tom, look out of the window—'

'I don't want to look out of the window. We're too high. We're much too high.'

'If we come down now, Tom, where will we be?'

'The sea. The sea. It's just sea all around now. We're completely out over the sea.'

'If I come down, we'll sink and drown, won't we? You just sit back and enjoy the view until we get to Paris.'

'Paris! We can't stay up here all the way to Paris. You don't even know the way to Paris.'

'Paris is in France. Everyone knows that. Those beaches and fields up ahead of us are France. We're almost in France already.'

Lucy and Jem leaned forward over the front seat, trying to get a better view of the beaches and fields of France. As soon as they did so, the front of the van dipped downwards so that there was nothing to see but sea and they were plunging towards it.

'Sit back! Get back!' yelled Dad. 'You're going make us crash.'

The children jumped back into their seats and felt their stomachs lurch into their throats as the van bounced up out of its dive and started to climb again.

'That was fun,' yelled Mum.

'That was not fun,' said Dad. 'Julie, please . . . that was a near-death experience.'

'Look! We're over the beach. We're in France. For the first time in its entire history, the Tooting family is abroad! All we've got to do now is find Paris.'

'Just please, very slowly, come back down,' said Dad. 'Come back down and we will buy a map and we will drive carefully and safely to wherever you want to go.'

'We want to go to Paris,' said Mum. 'It'll be far quicker to fly there. Why do we need a map? We're in the right country. Paris is large. We've seen pictures. We know what it looks like. I'm sure if we just keep going we'll spot it. Look, we can see everything from up here. Oh.'

The 'Oh' was because all at once she couldn't see anything at all.

Everything had gone grey. As though an unseen giant had wrapped the van in damp toilet roll.

The noise of the engine changed from a thrilling roar to a dull grumble.

'Where did the world go?' said Jem.

'I believe,' said Dad, 'we are inside a cloud. We need to duck down under it.'

'How do we do that?'

Then a terrible truth dawned on both parents. They were flying in some kind of plane but they only had the controls of a van. They could accelerate or brake. They could go left or right. They could indicate. Reverse. But there was no control for going higher or lower.

'Children,' said Dad, 'lean forward again. That worked last time.'

'No!' said Mum. 'We're over land. What if there are trees? Or power lines? Or the side of a hill? We need to go higher. We need to get above the clouds, not below them.'

'To the back of the van and lean backwards,' said Dad.

So Jem and Lucy jumped on to the back seat and leaned back as far as they could. Slowly the front of the van turned upwards. They could see the wisps of clouds falling past them like ghostly curtains.

When the last curtain was pulled back, everyone said, 'Oh!' and then, 'Oooh!' and Little Harry clapped. The sun had finally gone down and above the clouds was an endless, velvety night. Below them, the clouds were still flushed with the last red of sunset. But over their heads were endless clusters of hard, bright stars. They looked like catseyes marking out a million tangled roads. The planet Mars was like a faraway stop sign. Every now and then shooting stars appeared and disappeared, quick as racing cars. The children lay back in the seats, hypnotized by the wonder that was hidden away just above a cloudy night.

'No!' said Dad. 'Back to the middle. Lean forward. Lean forward. We're going too high . . . much too high.'

He was right. Already a fierce cold had got inside the van. It was biting into the children's hands and feet, and numbing their noses. They leaned forward until the van was just grazing the tops of the clouds – not sunset red any more but moonlight silver now. Dad jumped into the back and pulled extra jumpers and socks out of the cupboards to keep them warm.

'You know, Julie, it's dark,' he said. 'Don't you think you should turn on the headlights?'

'There isn't any other traffic up here, Tom.'

'How do you know that? We're up here and we didn't expect to be. How do you know there isn't some equally surprised French family heading the other way?'

'I never thought of that.' So she turned on the headlights, and their soft orange glow rolled out in front of them like a wide inviting road.

Soon the children began to feel tired. Lucy was the first to crawl off to her newly painted matt-black sleeping corner. Then Little Harry and finally Jem, who discovered that he still had in his pocket the tiny model plane that he had found at Bucklewing Corner. He thought how strange it was – a tiny plane flying inside another little plane – and that little plane flying inside the big ball of Earth's atmosphere and everyone bobbing about inside the atmosphere just like the plane was bobbing about inside the van and . . . thoughts like that sent him to sleep.

*

'Shall I drive now?' asked Dad. 'You must be feeling weary.'

'I'm not weary,' said Mum. 'But I know you'd love this. Take a turn.'

So they shuffled past each other and Dad took the wheel. Mum lay her head on his shoulder and he talked as they drifted through the stars.

'A few weeks ago this van was just another rusty Bargain of the Week in the corner of Unbeatable Motoring Bargains, and the engine was a piece of junk stuck up in a tree. And now, look, it's floating among the stars with its whole family on board.'

But though Mum had said she wasn't weary, she had already drifted off to sleep. Guiding the van through the night, with everyone sleeping peacefully around him, Dad felt like a super-guardian angel, carrying everyone safely into morning.

So he was pretty surprised when – what seemed like minutes later – he woke up in bright summer daylight, looking out across a city.

'Oh!' said Mum, rubbing her eyes. 'We've stopped. You found it! Clever old you!' Dad wasn't sure what she was talking about but took the praise anyway. 'Look, children. Daddy found Paris.'

'Paris?' said Lucy. 'Really?'

'Absolutely. I've dreamed about this day for years and years. Look, that river with all the different bridges, that's the Seine – oh, can we take a trip along it in one of those boats? – and that great cathedral with the two towers, on the island, that's Notre Dame – where

Quasimodo lived. Oh, nice work, Tom.'

'The reason I ask,' said Lucy, 'is that if this is Paris, right, where's the Eiffel Tower?'

'The Eiffel Tower! Oh I've always wanted to go up the Eiffel Tower. It's along the river somewhere. Let me see . . .' Mum twisted around in her seat.

'Wouldn't it be easier to just step out and look around and get our first lungful of Parisian air?' said Dad, opening the door, stepping out and completely and instantly vanishing.

'Where did Dad go?' said Jem.

'Daddy's hands!' shouted Little Harry, pointing excitedly to the floor by the driver's door. 'Daddy's hands! Daddy's hands!'

There indeed were Daddy's hands, or rather his fingers, clinging on desperately, the knuckles turning white. Dad was dangling by his fingertips on the edge of a thousand-foot drop, his eyes closed, his legs bicycling pointlessly in panic.

'Oh, Tom, what are you doing?' said Mum, grabbing one of his wrists. 'Look, children, your father is clinging by his fingertips on the edge of a thousand-foot drop. Honestly, he's such a show-off!'

Together they hauled Dad back inside. As soon as he could breathe he gasped, 'I've found the Eiffel Tower.'

'Well done, you.' Mum smiled, kissing him on the forehead. 'Where is it?'

'We are parked right on top of it.'

Indeed, the camper van was parked neatly and precisely on the edge of the roof of the uppermost observation deck, so when Dad stepped out he had fallen clean off the top of the Eiffel Tower. 'When you get out, children,' he said, 'please use the passenger-side doors.'

'The wings have gone,' said Jem.

'They pop back in when they're not in use,' said Dad. 'Sneezy is a convertible.'

'Scamper,' corrected Mum, but no one heard her because her voice was drowned out by a whirring, clanging sound like a cyclone full of tin trays. A helicopter was hovering right in front of them, so close that they could see the expressions of the men inside, and their uniforms. They were policemen. One of them picked up a microphone and said something. His amplified voice boomed and barked around them, but they mostly couldn't understand a word, because they mostly didn't speak French.

'I get the feeling they're angry,' shouted Jem.

'I'm sure they're just trying to be helpful,' said Mum. 'What makes you think they're angry?'

'The ones behind us are pointing guns.'

'Bang!' yelled Little Harry.

Mum and Dad looked in the rear-view mirror. Armed police were climbing out of a hatch on to the roof behind them, and pointing their guns at the Tooting family camper van.

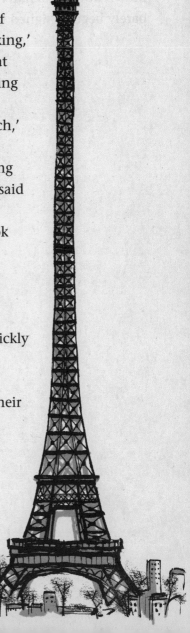

'Bang!
Bang!' yelled
Little Harry.

'They are saying that the top of
the Eiffel Tower is strictly no parking,'
said Lucy. 'And they're saying that
the Republic of France takes parking
restrictions very seriously.'

'I didn't know you spoke French,'
said Dad.

'What did you think I was doing
when I was locked in my room?' said
Lucy. 'Polishing my nails?'

'Well, your nails always do look
unusually well polished.'

'I was studying stuff, including
French.'

The police were still yelling.

'They say we're not moving quickly
enough.'

Everyone clambered out and
walked towards the police with their
hands up.

'Oh, wait!' said Dad 'The
keys . . .' But as he grabbed the
hefty, oily crank handle, the
police yelled louder and
waved their guns.

'Dad, they think you're going to use that to assault them and if you don't drop it they're going to shoot. Mown down in a hail of bullets in Paris when my life has barely begun!' sighed Lucy. 'How beautiful.'

Mum had often daydreamed about going to Paris. She had pictured herself wafting along the river bank, browsing the book stalls and the flower market, drinking coffee in the cafés. She had never once pictured herself being handcuffed and shoved into the service lift of the Eiffel Tower by a troop of armed policemen.

'This is so much more exciting than I imagined,' she said. 'Children, you're very lucky. This is a side of Paris that tourists never normally see.'

'*Vite bougez!*' shouted the biggest armed officer as the lift doors opened.

A tall man with grey hair and a pipe came towards them. 'Good morning,' he said. 'I am the most important police officer in Paris, and before this day is through I am going to find out what you are playing at. Are you terrorists? Protesters? Pathetic self-publicists? Or part of some clever criminal conspiracy? I will know. Follow me to the police car.'

They did try to follow him to the police car but by now hundreds of people were gathered under the tower and as soon as they saw the Tootings they rushed forward, taking photographs and shouting questions.

'Monsieur Tooting, you have parked on the tower as a protest against cars and pollution, *n'est-ce pas*?'

'*Non*! It's a protest about the lack of parking spaces in Paris. *C'est vrai*, Monsieur Tooting?'

'It's an insult to the Eiffel Tower and to French civic engineering.'

'Imbeciles! Monsieur Tooting is not protesting at all. It's a work of art – isn't it, Monsieur Tooting? A camper van on top of the Eiffel Tower. *C'ést élegant*. Surreal. Paris loves you, Monsieur Tooting! Down with the police! Down with the police! Down with the police!'

When he heard this the Most Important Police Officer tried to shove Dad and Mum into the waiting squad car. Dad turned round to the crowd and raised his hands for quiet.

'Lucy, can you translate for me?' he asked.

'*Bien sûr, mon père*,' said Lucy, and she did. Dad thanked everyone for coming and promised everyone that he wasn't a criminal. 'I have parked there,' he said, 'because the first time I went out with my wife we saw a film. A film set in Paris. Since then our hearts have been entwined with each other but also with Paris. We have never been to Paris until today. I parked there because I wanted her to wake up with Paris all around her. I wanted

ODIN'S KISS

to spread Paris at her feet like a big Paris-y towel at the end of a long bath.'

For a moment no one said anything. Then someone started to clap. Then everyone started to clap. Except the Most Important Police Officer, who wiped away a tear and sniffed. 'I have investigated many crimes of passion,' he said in French, 'but I have never seen passion like this.'

'What did he say?' said Dad.

'He said something revolting,' said Lucy.

'What did he say?'

'He said you and Mum were romantic. It was disgusting. It really upset me.'

'I think that's quite nice,' said Mum. 'And also true. He's obviously a good detective. He got that right.'

'Kiss her!' yelled someone in the crowd. 'Kiss your beautiful wife.'

'Kiss her!' cried someone else. And 'Kiss her!' shouted everyone else.

DOISNEAU'S KISS

'Please don't,' said Lucy. 'Oh. Too late.'

Mum and Dad kissed and a thousand mobile phones filmed them doing it.

THE TOOTINGS' KISS!

'Paris loves the Tootings!' shouted the crowd.

'Am I still alive?' asked Lucy. 'Because I feel like I've died and woken up in hell.'

'Please get into the police car,' said the Most Important Police Officer.

'Are we still under arrest?' said Mum. 'After all that kissing?'

'No,' said the Most Important Police Officer. 'I would like to offer you my car and my driver for the rest of the day. He will drive you to wherever you want to go here in Paris. You are Guests of the City.'

Mum kissed Dad again and Lucy said to the police officer in French, 'Honestly, it would be better for everyone if you just arrested them.'

At that moment another car pulled up in front of them and a man with big hair and a big microphone jumped out, quickly followed by a woman with a film camera.

'Monsieur Tooting,' bawled the man, shoving the microphone through the car window, 'I am Jean Charles Roué, presenter of the most popular television emission in France – *Car Stupide*. This is our camera person – Ernestine.'

Ernestine was a tiny woman with a massive camera balanced on her shoulder. '*Bonsoir*,' she said. 'Please to look into the lens when you are speaking.'

'Our viewers would love to know how you achieve such a magnificent piece of parking,' said Monsieur Roué.

The lens of Ernestine's camera stared at Dad like a blank, accusing eye. He couldn't look into it. He looked into the air and shrugged, which only made people like him even more, because it looked surprisingly French.

'Monsieur Tooting,' said the Most Important Police Officer, 'has parked his van for love. Love is a mystery. So you must allow him to retain the mystery of his parking.'

'Of course. But if I can only ask . . . *how are you going to get down again?*'

Another shrug from Dad – he couldn't speak in French but he was enjoying shrugging in it.

'If I can only ask then . . . WHEN are you going to bring it down?'

Dad tried to shrug again, but the Most Important Police Officer answered for him instead. 'Tonight,' he said. '*Ce soir*. Parking on top of the Eiffel Tower is one thing – charming, picturesque, romantic – but taking up residence there is another thing entirely. He will move the motor car down this evening, after he and Madame Tooting have appreciated Paris.'

Monsieur Roué turned to Ernestine's camera. 'People of France, you heard it first on *Caaaar Stupide*. This very evening, Monsieur Tooting will perform the extraordinary feat of removing a VW camper van from the top of the Eiffel Tower. Only he knows how he is going to do it.'

Jem was wondering, How will Dad get it down? We know it can fly, he thought, but we don't know how to make it fly. It flew when Mum was driving in Dover, but she drove about half a mile before it took off. We can't do that on the roof of the Eiffel Tower. There isn't room.

The wings opened when it fell off the cliff, thought Dad, so maybe they'd open if I just drove off the edge of the tower. Maybe. It's not something I want to risk. I mean, what if they don't open?

'Monsieur Tooting,' bawled Monsueur Roué, 'how will you do it? Our viewers are desperate to know.'

'Well, you know –' another French shrug – 'what goes

up must come down, ha ha.' He winked at Jem, as though he had a secret plan.

Great, thought Jem. He's obviously got a secret plan. I'll just relax and enjoy the afternoon.

'Tune into *Caaaaaaaar Stupide* tonight, when Monsieur Tooting will reveal all.'

The first place that the police car took the Tootings was the famous and beautiful cathedral of Notre Dame, where the archbishop himself showed them round and even let Little Harry swing on the bells in the bell tower, which no one had been allowed to do since the days of Quasimodo. They thanked him profusely and he said, 'It's nothing really. Though, if you were to wish to tell me – discreetly – how you are going to get your van down, I would be honoured to hear.'

'The word today,' said Dad, 'is *just wait and see.*'

'That's actually four words,' said the archbishop.

'He hasn't even told us yet,' said Mum, 'but he's got an idea. We can tell. Isn't that right, Jem?'

'That's right,' said Jem.

Dad tried not to think about it, but the truth is that wherever you go in Paris you can see the Eiffel Tower (except from the Eiffel Tower, of course) and every time Dad saw it, he was reminded that the Hour of Doom was coming closer.

'I'll be watching *Car Stupide* tonight,' said the archbishop. 'I never miss it.'

*

The archbishop put the Tootings on to a special boat – a Bateau Mouche – which took them up the river to the Louvre. On board the boat a little orchestra played just for them. All along the river banks and in passing boats, people waved and threw flowers.

'This is so embarrassing,' said Lucy.

'Actually I quite like it,' said Jem.

The captain asked Dad if he'd like to try steering. As he guided the boat between the barges, under the bridges, past the great buildings of Paris, with his wife's hand on his shoulder and the breeze in his face, he sighed, 'I could live like this.' Every time he looked up, he saw that tower, thrusting into the sky like a huge blade that was about to fall.

Inside the Louvre, the Man in Charge took the *Mona Lisa* down from the wall just so Mum could get a better look at it. After that he let Mum pose with it for photographs.

She held it next to her face and tried to copy the *Mona Lisa*'s smile.

'You could be twins,' said the Man in Charge.

'Good grief!' said Lucy.

'How can we thank you?' said Dad.

'Well, you can tell me what all of Paris is burning to know,' said the Man in Charge.

'No,' said Dad.

Back on the river, waving to the cheering crowds, Mum said, 'When I was daydreaming about my trip to Paris, this is exactly how I imagined it. I wish it could go on forever.'

'So do I,' said Jem as they floated back towards the Eiffel Tower. 'Look – power steering, an onboard computer that tells you your average speed and fuel consumption, a camera that shows you exactly what's behind you when you're docking – why can't we have a car like that?'

'Oh, look! The Eiffel Tower!' said Mum. 'I didn't know you could see it from here.'

You can see it from everywhere, thought Dad. Even when you close your eyes.

As the sun set over the Seine, the Tootings arrived at the tower. A great cheer went up as Mum stepped out on to the bank.

'Tom, there are hundreds of people here – thousands in fact. Just for us.'

'I know,' said Dad.

Cameras flashed like fireworks. People waved and shouted as though it was a football match. Monsieur Roué and Ernestine emerged from the crowd. He spoke into his big microphone. 'Paris holds its breath. Monsieur Tooting and his family are about to climb the tower and reveal the mystery of how they are going to get the van down. Monsieur Tooting, on behalf of *Car Stupide*, we ask one last time . . . how are you going to do it?'

'I'm afraid how we will do it is a secret between Sneezy and the Tooting family.'

'*Excusez-moi*, who is Sneezy?'

'It's just the name we call the van.'

'No, it's not,' said Lucy.

'The children thought it up,' said Dad.

'Most certainly did not,' snarled Lucy.

'Little Harry likes it,' said Dad.

'Yuk!' said Little Harry.

'OK, *Car Stupide* viewers, let's go!' yelled Monsieur Roué, and he led the Tooting family through the crowd towards the tower. Reporters called out questions as they passed:

'Mademoiselle Tooting, is it true that your father cruelly made you carry the pieces of his van up the steps of the tower all night so that he could assemble it on the roof?'

'Is it true that you are not going to move the van at all but you're going to live in it as a protest about the lack of homes for working people here in Paris?'

'Is it true that the van was carried up there by hot-air balloon?'

'Is it the case that the van is in fact a balloon disguised as a van?'

'Is it true that you are aliens?'

'Is it true that the van is in fact not a van at all but a gigantic cake and tonight it will be cut into slices and we will all get some?'

'Madame Tooting, would you accept this gift from me? It is a sculpture of your whole family in the form of larger-than-average jelly babies. Here is you in raspberry and this is your son in lime and so on. It is a work of art you inspired in me . . .'

The lift seemed to take an amazingly long time to get to the top of the tower.

'The lift seems to be taking an amazingly long time,' said Dad, 'to get to the top of the tower.'

'That's good,' said Monsieur Roué. 'It'll all add to the suspense for our viewers on *Car Stupide*.'

'It takes a long time,' said Ernestine, 'because it's such a very long way up.'

'And soon, viewers – just imagine,' said Monsieur Roué into the camera, 'Monsieur Tooting will be standing on top of it.'

'Yes, just imagine.'

'Of course, he's not the first person to stand on the top. The pioneer of the parachute – Franz Reichelt – he jumped off the tower in 1912 to test his invention.'

'Nice to know that someone jumped off and survived,' said Dad.

'I never said he survived,' said Monsieur Roué. 'His invention failed that particular test and he was smashed to pieces by his fall.'

'Ah,' said Dad. 'Well, you live and learn.'

'Yes,' said Monsieur Roué. 'Of course, you don't necessarily live.'

The observation deck of the Eiffel Tower is a beautiful, curving room with fabulous views across Paris. If you look through its windows at night, the city lights look like ropes of diamonds and sapphires thrown on a velvet cushion.

The Tooting family did not look out of the windows. They followed Monsieur Roué to a narrow wooden door just around the corner from the lifts. If you've ever been to the Eiffel Tower you probably didn't notice this door at all and if you did you probably thought it led to a cupboard filled with mops and brushes. It doesn't. It leads to a narrow staircase that goes up to the roof of the observation deck.

'This is called the Solomon Door, after a cat.' The keyhole was clogged with spiders' webs and dead flies. 'Solomon was a white Persian cat who came to live here while the tower was being built. The builders and the painters adopted him, but he was always getting out on to the roof and they kept having to go and rescue him. Until you Tootings arrived, I don't believe that this door had been opened since the second-to-last time Solomon climbed out, which was in 1892.' Monsieur Roué had to bash the door hard with his shoulder to get it open.

'Why the second-to-last time?' asked Jem.

'Because the last time he did it, no one needed to go and get Solomon back.'

'Why? Oh. I see.'

'The whole three hundred metres,' said Monsieur Roué. 'If you know where to look, you can still see the dent in the pavement down below. Ah. Here we are.' Finally the door creaked open. A blast of freezing wind blew in and Monsieur Roué led the Tooting family through the practically never-opened door and up the barely-climbed-in-a-hundred-and-twenty-years ladder to the roof of the Eiffel Tower.

At the top of the ladder was a hatch which opened out on a kind of metal platform with a fence around it, and beyond the fence the roof of the observation deck spread out around them like a big red field. In the middle of the field a huge radio antenna, like the skeleton of a giant Christmas tree, spiked into the starry night. There, beyond that, right against the edge of the roof, was the camper van.

Monsieur Roué and Ernestine stepped to one side.

'Sadly, viewers,' he said into the camera, '*Car Stupide* cannot go any nearer than this due to health and safety. But fear not, because Ernestine has a long lens so if the family does plunge to its doom, you will get a ringside view. Monsieur Tooting, if I may ask, are you worried about plunging to your doom?'

'Worried? Us? We laugh at danger, don't we, children?' said Mum.

Little Harry laughed and Dad tried to join in. Then

they clambered over the protective fence on to the roof of the Eiffel Tower.

The roof of the Eiffel Tower is a lot more frightening at night than it is in the morning sunshine. The wind comes at you from every direction, whipping through the antenna girders, pushing you from this side and that, like a mob of bullies with freezing hands. It was all the Tootings could do to stay upright. Their little blue-and-cream camper van was just a few yards away from them, but those few feet of open space were a kind of channel through which the wind rushed like a river of freezing air. They felt that if they took one step towards it, they would be swept off the roof and into the city below. So they stood with their backs to the biggest girder, holding on, saying nothing.

'So,' said Mum eventually, 'what's the plan, Tom?'

'Yes,' said Jem, 'how are you going to get it down?'

'We all know that this van can fly,' said Dad, 'so the plan is to get her to fly.'

'Yes,' said Jem. 'But we don't know how to do that. The buttons on the dashboard don't match up with the buttons on the engine. They say radio and cigarette lighter and indicator lights, not altitude and wind speed. We don't even know how to make the wings pop out.'

'Well,' said Dad, 'would anyone like a larger-than-average jelly baby? Look, they're in the shape of our family. Look . . . I'm the raspberry one.'

'Not just now,' said Mum. 'Just now we want to know how we are going to get down. Alive.'

'Well, if you remember, when she went over the cliff in Dover, the wings just opened. I think the wings are probably some kind of emergency device, so all we have to do is create an emergency.'

'Found them! Found them!' yelled Little Harry.

No one took any notice.

'You mean,' said Lucy, 'all we have to do is go off a cliff or fall off the top of the Eiffel Tower?'

'That's right,' said Dad. 'Anyone want to come with me? Or shall I go on my own?'

'Found them!' yelled Little Harry again.

'No!' said Mum. 'No one is going to do that. Jump off the Tower? No.' She let go of the girder and put her arms around all three children. 'I'd rather pay the parking fine.'

'I think it's just a matter of having a bit of faith in Sneezy,' said Dad.

'No one on Earth would put their faith in something called Sneezy,' said Lucy. 'Or Scamper,' she added before Mum got the chance.

'I don't want any of you to take any risks,' said Dad. 'That's why I'm going to do this myself. I'm going to drive Sneezy off the roof, and if she flies I'll be back.'

'No, Tom, that can't be right,' said Mum. But Dad was already pushing through the wind, towards the van. 'Tom, come back!'

'At least leave us the jelly babies,' said Lucy. 'They'll be no good to you if you plummet to your doom.'

Dad was at the van. He put the family of larger-than-average jelly babies on the passenger seat. He braced himself to go around the front to crank the starter . . .

He distinctly heard the *parp* of a car horn.

There couldn't be another car up here, could there? He looked around. He couldn't see one.

The *parp* sounded again. It seemed to come from somewhere in the cab. He looked around and saw that the raspberry larger-than-average jelly baby was glowing. The car horn sound was a mobile-phone ringtone. The jelly babies weren't sweets at all. They were mobile phones. 'Hello?' said Dad, picking it up.

'Hello. Mr Tooting?'

'Yes. Who's that?'

'Mr Tooting, what's your favourite ever car?'

'Me? I don't know. Maybe the Aston Martin DB5. Who is this?'

'So . . . not a VW camper van from the 1960s then?'

'Well, I like this van but . . . Who is this?'

'Who am I? I'm your stroke of luck, Mr Tooting, because tonight I'm ringing to offer you a shiny little Aston Martin DB5 just for you.'

'*What*?'

'In exchange for your heap of rust.'

'Really?'

'Best of all, Mr Tooting, I will collect. I will come over and take the camper van off your hands. You don't need to worry about how to get it down off the Eiffel Tower. I, Tiny Jack, will do it for you. How does that sound?'

'That sounds very nice, thank you, er, Mr Jack . . .' said Dad.

'But?'

'It's a kind offer, a very kind offer. I'd love to accept it really. But there are five of us and a lot of luggage. We wouldn't fit in a little sports car. We need a camper van.'

'OK. I'll get you a new camper van.'

'We like this one.'

'Let me get this clear. I'm offering you your pick of the most elegant, stylish, enviable cars in the world, and you won't swap it for your ridiculous rustbucket?'

'Sneezy may be just a pile of rust to you, Mr Whatever Your Name Is. But we are proud of her. We rebuilt her. We painted and polished her. Now, look, the whole of Paris is watching her. We're proud of her and we're proud of ourselves.'

'Sneezy? What's Sneezy?'

'It's the name of this vehicle.'

The voice of Monsieur Roué came booming through a loudspeaker. 'Monsieur Tooting, what is happening? Paris is waiting. We can hear you. Ernestine has a long-range microphone.'

Before Dad could answer Tiny Jack snapped, 'I've just offered this fool anything. Anything he wants in exchange for his rusty old van.'

'Monsieur Tooting, will you take that offer?'

Dad looked around him. At the lights of Paris. At Mum waving cheerily at him. At the children standing there expectantly. At the beautiful interior of the van he and Jem had refurbished. 'The thing is,' he said, 'I already have everything I want.' Then, bracing himself again, he went round to the front of the van. He heard Ernestine sigh, 'Beautiful. *Car Stupide* loves the Tooting family. Paris loves the Tooting family.'

Proudly Dad turned the crank handle as hard as he

could. Turned it once. Turned it twice . . . Nothing.

The engine didn't roar.

Didn't even cough.

Didn't so much as splutter.

Or sneeze.

Most of all, it didn't start.

He tried again, turning it harder than ever this time.

Nothing.

Again.

Nothing. Then there was a beep.

It was a different jelly baby. The lime one. When Dad picked it up a little screen flickered into life in its stomach. On the screen Dad could see a man sitting on a chair. A man whose legs barely came to the edge of the chair's cushion and whose hands didn't reach the seat's arms.

'Tiny Jack?' said Dad slowly. 'You really are tiny, aren't you?'

'You just said you were proud of the van and proud of yourselves. Ha! Still proud now that it doesn't even start?'

'Well, you know, it's cold up here and damp. The engine is nearly a hundred years old.'

'I know how old that engine is! Don't try to tell me about that engine!' Tiny Jack began howling and crying and pulling his hair. 'Give me your van now. I want it now! NOW! NOW! NOWWWWWWWWWWW!'

'Tiny Jack,' said Dad, 'do you know what we do in our house when people behave badly? We ignore them.'

With that he dropped the phone out of the window.

Straight away the phone started to ring again. 'Answer me!' it yelled. 'Don't ignore me! It's not fair!' It buzzed around on the roof of the tower like a big angry cockroach.

Dad didn't answer the phone. He had something more interesting to do.

When Jem had realized how important it was to listen to the engine, he had started listening to people too. Jem remembered that when they first arrived back on the roof, Little Harry kept shouting, 'Found them! Found them!' They all ignored him then, thinking it was just some baby nonsense. Jem decided to listen to his little brother. So when Little Harry said, 'There they are!' Jem looked to where Little Harry was pointing. There were two big brass lamps fitted to the girders of the Eiffel Tower. They were directed upwards, lighting a sign advertising motor oil. With Dad busy in the van, Jem edged nearer to the lamps, holding on to the wires and struts of the tower. He looked closely at the lights. They were brass car headlights – big, old-fashioned, with a slot in the back where they were fitted to the sign. When Jem looked closer, he gasped. For there, engraved on the brass fittings in lovely curvy writing, just like the writing on the plaque on the engine, was that name again – Zborowski. These were no ordinary headlights. These were the lamps that went with the engine.

Carefully Jem tugged at them. They lifted smoothly off the metal girders, and it was easy to unplug the wires at the back. Jem picked one up – it was warm and very heavy – but he managed to carry it over to the van, open the door and show it to Dad.

'Zborowski,' he said.

Dad looked at Jem. Then he nodded. 'Let's give it a go.'

So Dad and Jem slotted the lights into the brackets on each side of the radiator. They looked completely at home there because

they were at home there. The front of the van looked more like a face than ever now that those big, round eye-shaped headlamps were in place.

The word today,' said Dad, 'is *Let's hope she starts now that she's got her old headlights back.*'

'That's actually twelve words,' said Jem.

Dad didn't even have to turn the crank handle. He had barely fitted it into the slot when the engine roared like a happy elephant. The headlights flashed on and off three times very fast, as though the car was blinking, or trying her new eyes for size.

When Dad clambered into the driving seat Jem naturally tried to follow him. 'Oh no you don't,' said Dad, shutting the door in his face.

'But, Dad . . .' called Jem.

'If I'm going to drive over a thousand-foot drop, I'm going to do it by myself. I'm not taking anyone with me.' He revved the engine, slipped the brakes, put it in gear and – as Jem stood and watched him – drove the van off the top of the Eiffel Tower.

'Dad!' yelled Jem.

'Tom!' screamed Mum.

'Fly!' burbled Little Harry.

Then there was silence.

The lights twinkled.

The wind blew.

Jem looked back at Mum. She was still holding tight to Little Harry and to Lucy.

Then . . .

Boom!

There was another rush of wind – but an oily, warm wind this time as, wings and all, the van went soaring up over Jem's head and flew once round the aerial of the Eiffel Tower. The cheering down below was so loud that Jem could hear it a thousand feet away.

After flying once round the tower, Dad brought the van in to land. 'Jump in, everyone,' he said. 'She's running better than ever.'

Everyone climbed in. The engine sounded just as powerful as before, but smoother, less sneezy, as though it was happier. As the van launched itself into the air, its nose swung from side to side, sweeping the night with her dear old headlights.

'Sneezy's showing off!' said Dad.

'It doesn't even sound like a sneeze now,' said Lucy. This was true. The engine made a busy, metal noise and then a couple of sharp little explosions, which everyone knew was the pistons firing with beautiful regularity.

'It's more of a *chitty chitty* sound,' said Jem.

'Bang! Bang!' yelled Little Harry, as the van drew a big, graceful spiral round the Eiffel Tower.

'Chitty Chitty.'

'Bang Bang.'

'Now that,' said Lucy, 'is a good name.'

Jem looked down at the strings and knots and clusters of light spreading out below. They were not flying as high as a plane – so high that all you could see were clouds. They were flying just a bit higher than the tallest building imaginable. He could easily see the woodlands and motorways, the fields and the hypermarkets, the boating lakes and big car parks, the spires and the schools. He felt like a bird. He thought of all the people down there – the families watching TV, the children reading in bed, the people out walking their dogs, or on their way home from work at the end of a long day, or trudging out to work at the beginning of a night shift. Thousands of people. Thousands of different lives, and none of them knew that the Tooting family was skimming high above their heads.

'We are now flying over Orléans,' said Lucy, who had a map feature called YouFinder on her mobile phone.

'All we have to do is head south,' said Dad, 'then turn

left at Africa and we can't miss Cairo. Just look at this, everyone.' Through the windscreen, they could see the two cones of orange light made by the headlamps. At Limoges the children pulled the curtains and went to bed.

By the time YouFinder pointed out Lyon, Mum was sleeping too and Dad, at the wheel, was the only one awake. By Marseille he was feeling sleepy himself. He yawned. Dawn was breaking on the horizon.

'Dad,' said Jem from his bunk. 'Can I drive?'

'Of course not. You have to be seventeen to drive.'

'That's on roads. This is in the air.'

'That only makes it worse. What if we crashed?'

'Why would I crash? I more or less built this van. I know exactly how it works.'

'I said no. Now please wake your mother.'

Jem tugged the floral curtains open just above Mum's bed. She stretched and said, 'Oh!' because there is something especially cosy about pulling open the floral curtains in your camper van and finding the Mediterranean sea shining hundreds of feet below you and seabirds twirling all around you. Especially if the kettle has just boiled.

Everything was peaceful and bright. Lucy woke up and rummaged around for her pot of black paint. It was time to give her corner another coat.

'Can I open the window?' asked Jem as they flew over a ferry boat.

'Of course,' said Mum.

Jem leaned out and waved. The passengers on deck waved back. The captain gave them a toot on the horn. Unfortunately ferry horns use steam from the engines, so Jem was quickly covered in soot and grime.

He was still getting the soot out of his eyes when the rest of the family started screaming.

'Where did they come from?'

'They're coming towards us!'

'What is *that*?'

'Make it stop!'

'Go higher, go higher! We're going to crash!'

'Reverse! Reverse!'

Jem looked up just in time to see a wall of rock and snow rushing towards them. 'Is that a mountain?' he said.

'You are now in,' said YouFinder, 'the Atlas Mountains.'

'No one mentioned the Atlas Mountains to me,' said Mum, who was driving now. 'This is supposed to be

Africa. I thought it was going to be sunshine and giraffes, not rocks and snow.'

'The Atlas Mountains, current height – four thousand one hundred and seventy metres,' said YouFinder, and added helpfully, 'Your current height – one hundred and seventy metres. Thank you for your time.'

'Go higher!' yelled Dad. 'Go a lot higher.'

'Chitty Chitty High High!' laughed Little Harry.

'We can't go that high!' said Mum calmly. 'I'll turn back.' She pulled really hard on the wheel. As soon as Chitty turned side on, the whole camper van rolled over completely, sending cups and books and bedding everywhere. Mum was trying to drive with a duvet on her head. When she managed to peep out from under it, the mountains were still heading towards them.

'The problem we have here,' said Lucy, 'is wind turbulence. You see, the wind comes over the mountains and a combination of air-pressure fluctuation and temperature gradient sucks it downwards. It's like a river of wind flowing down the mountain. It's called a downdraught.'

'Just give me the headlines,' said Mum, still tugging at Chitty's steering wheel.

'OK, to put it in two words,' said Lucy, 'we're doomed.'

'Can't we just turn back?' said Dad.

'I'm trying. You try. It's as if the van just doesn't want to—' They swapped seats.

'There!' yelled Jem. 'Over there! Look!'

There was a valley. Over to the left and down below

them. A narrow valley. But definitely a valley.

'If we could get to that, then maybe we could get through without going higher . . .'

Dad tried to turn Chitty left, but once again, as soon as she was side on to the wind, she rolled right over and caused another Mug and Duvet Avalanche. He tried again to turn towards the valley, but as soon as he pulled the steering wheel Chitty's engine snarled, as if she was telling him not to.

'Just nudge her a bit,' said Jem. 'You have to listen to her.'

Dad did as Jem suggested, and Chitty moved just a tiny bit nearer to the valley, then floated for a while, her wings fluttering. She was shuddering but not moving much – like a kite in a high wind. Dad nudged her again and she purred again. And again. And again. Inch by inch they got nearer to the valley without losing any more height. It seemed to Jem that every time they gained an inch, Chitty's engine purred a little louder as though she was telling them how pleased she was. Then she coughed, an annoyed, pointed kind of cough.

'Something's wrong,' said Jem. 'She sounds like she did before she got her headlamps back.'

'Headlamps wouldn't affect the engine,' said Dad.

Jem could still hear the coughing and the spluttering.

'I'm not sure if anyone is interested in indicators and gauges and so on,' said Lucy, 'but I'm fairly sure that red light there means we have no petrol. As I believe I mentioned earlier, we are doomed.'

As she said this, Chitty made one last shift to the left

and finally she was facing the entrance to the valley. As though a switch had been flicked, the wind stopped, and the van dropped like a stone through the freezing air, plunging towards the jagged rocks below.

The Tooting family didn't fall as fast as the van. They lay with their backs on the ceiling, their heads pinned to the roof, their stomachs still somewhere thirty metres above them, watching the cliffs and boulders stream past outside the window when suddenly . . .

They were hurtling through the valley as though they had been shot out of a catapult.

What happened?

Lucy explained. 'The valley – actually a pass between two of the highest points in the Atlas range – slopes steeply from north to south and forms a kind of corridor linking the mild air of the sea side with the hot air of the Sahara Desert on the other side. The resulting pressure gradient sucks air from north to south, just as at the summit the temperature gradient was pushing air from south to north. At the summit there was a downdraught. In the valley there's an updraught. Chitty has got caught in the updraught – a current of air that is more or less rushing the van from the mountains to the desert. You see, what happens often is—'

'Lucy,' said Dad, 'how do you know so much about meteorology?'

'What do you think I was doing in my bedroom all these years?'

'You did say you were studying French. But I thought

you were mostly sulking and staring out of the window.'

'I was staring out of the window. At the weather.'

The valley was so narrow, Chitty's wing tips were almost touching each side. They were flying through an ancient, colossal tunnel. Then they were out, soaring over a dry sandy plain, as though they'd been spat out of a massive stone pea-shooter.

'How are we flying if we've got no petrol?' said Mum.

'We're not flying, we're gliding,' said Jem. 'Listen.'

There was nothing – no sound from the engine at all. Or from the wind. They drifted silently over hills and sand dunes, noiselessly passing over a road and then a walled city. From the air it looked like the best toy fort ever. Beyond the city walls, something that looked like a gigantic colourful quilt spread out in the sand.

'A market!' said Mum. 'Look, those cloths are the roofs of the stalls. And those splashes of red are . . . gosh.'

They could see now that some of the colours they had seen from the air were piles of fresh spices, chillies, oranges, grapes, figs, olives. They were gliding just above the stalls and the shoppers. No one saw them. No one looked up. Everyone was much too busy choosing and weighing and haggling and gossiping. No one had time to notice a low-gliding camper van as it brushed the tops of the palm trees.

Then they were in the desert. Sand dunes rolled beneath them like slow, golden waves and Chitty followed the contours – rising high over the peaks, sweeping low into the valleys, riding the thermals of hot air as though the Sahara was one vast, gentle fairground ride. For hours and hours the view didn't vary. Once they saw some kind of fox scurrying down a dune. Just a little fox with unusually big ears, but after so long without seeing any living creature at all, it seemed as magical and impossible as a unicorn. Later they saw a jeep with a pair of bored-looking camels tethered to the back of it, their shadows waving on the hot sand like strange trees. There was no sign of a driver.

Then it went dark.

Just like that.

It was light.

Then it was dark.

'Headlights,' yelled Dad. 'Put the headlights on, darling.'

'What happened?'

'There are no sunsets in the desert,' explained Lucy,

'due to the low horizon. The sun appears to drop very rapidly, giving the appearance of instant night. Also there are no petrol fumes and so on to create that afterglow we see when the sun sets back home.'

'So it's nothing strange or worrying then?'

'It's perfectly normal, but it is worrying. If you remember, we have no petrol. For the last few hours we haven't been flying, we've been gliding, using thermals of hot air rising from the sand. Now that the sun has gone down, everything will cool down and so we can expect to . . . oh.'

'Oh!'

'Ow!'

There was a terrible jolt. Chitty had run into a bank of sand.

'Is everyone all right?'

Everyone was all right.

'For the moment,' said Lucy. 'But we are in a camper van in the middle of the desert with no fuel, limited water and no emergency food rations.'

'That is true,' said Mum. 'Does anyone have a plan?'

'What about . . . ?' Dad thought for a moment. 'What about coffee and pancakes?'

'Perhaps we shouldn't use too much water,' said Mum, 'not if we're stranded in the middle of the desert.'

'Shhhh,' said Jem. 'Listen.'

'What?'

'Can't you hear? Voices.'

There were voices – slightly distant, but definitely

voices – laughing, talking, arguing, singing, old and young voices.

'If we're all alone in the middle of the desert, how can there be voices?' asked Mum.

'Clearly,' said Lucy, 'we've all gone mad from fear. Now we're hallucinating.'

'Scared!' yelled Little Harry.

'Now, now, don't be scared, Little Harry,' said Mum. 'Ghosts can't hurt you.'

'Scared! Scared!' yelled Little Harry, pointing at the windscreen.

Mum followed his gaze and gave a yelp of fear. Then Dad, then Lucy and then Jem all looked where Little Harry had been pointing and all gasped in fear and horror. A face was staring in through the windscreen. A cold, unblinking, unseeing face. A huge face. A face the size of a cliff.

Dad covered his eyes with his hands. 'Has it gone?' he said. He seemed to think that if he could stop himself seeing it, then it would stop being there.

'No,' said Lucy, 'it hasn't gone. And it's not going. It hasn't gone anywhere for thousands of years. Look.'

Dad peeked. Then Mum. They looked more closely.

'It's . . .' said Dad.

'Yes, it is,' said Lucy. 'This van has parked itself right in front of the Sphinx. In Egypt. We couldn't see it when we first landed because it was all in darkness. Then the moon rose.'

'And the voices . . .'

'. . . are people who've come to see the Sphinx by moonlight.'

'According to YouFinder,' said Lucy, checking her phone, 'the Sphinx is ten kilometres from Cairo by road, so we're not in the middle of the desert at all. In fact we are conveniently situated for water, petrol, food and all amenities.'

'So,' said Dad, 'coffee, anyone? And what about those pancakes?'

Jem lay on his bed listening to the homely sounds of eggs being cracked and the kettle being boiled, smelling the rich perfume of Dad's coffee. If he closed his eyes he felt like he was back in Zborowski Terrace, but if he opened them, he was looking at the moonlit Sphinx and the candles and campfires of its visitors.

'Errm . . . is anyone expecting a visitor?'

Lucy had been too excited about seeing the Sphinx to wait for coffee and pancakes. So she'd put on her shoes and her coat and slid open the door of the van and found a surprise. Someone was waiting to come in. A dozen people, in fact. All waiting in an orderly line, chatting. The moment they saw Lucy, they pushed closer to the van and started yelling things at her.

'What's going on? What do they want?' said Mum. 'Have you parked illegally again, Tom?'

'I don't know,' said Dad. 'I don't speak Sphinxese.'

'Arabic,' Lucy corrected him. 'They think we are a snack van. This man in the stripes wants two coffees and two pancakes. The one with the beard is asking if you do tea . . .'

Dad was carrying Lucy's pancakes. Before Lucy had even looked at them, the man at the front of the queue had taken them and was eating them and giving Dad a big thumbs-up and a small banknote with a picture of the pyramids on it. The rest of the queue squeezed closer while the man with the pancakes seemed to be describing their finer points, explaining how flat they were and crispy round the edges but squashy in the middle, with maybe just a slight sweetness that really made them the best he'd ever eaten. There was more shouting. Lucy said, 'Some of them are asking if we have ice cream to go with the pancakes.'

Dad stared at Lucy. 'Lucy,' he said, 'do you speak Arabic?'

'*Shwaya.*'

'Where did you learn to speak Arabic?'

'In my bedroom.'

'French. Meteorology. Egyptology. Arabic . . . And all this time we thought you were just on Facebook.'

'I was. A lot of my Facebook friends are bilingual Egyptian meteorologists.'

'Well, can you use your Arabic to tell these people that we are not a snack van. We are a family home.'

'Egyptians,' said Lucy, 'attach very great importance to hospitality. If you tell them this is your home, they will think you are inviting them to free pancakes. At least as long as they think we are a snack van, they will give us money.'

'Which we need,' said Jem, 'for petrol.' He handed his pancakes to the next person in the queue in exchange for a fistful of tiny coins.

So the Tooting family spent the night cracking eggs, whisking batter, flipping and, most of all, selling pancakes. Mum and Lucy put out the deckchairs so that customers could sit and talk and ask for second helpings. The moonlit Sphinx looked down on them all as they passed the pancakes out. Much later, Dad and Jem walked across the cool sands in search of a petrol station. They found a single pump with a boy sitting next to it and some goats. The boy was eating one of the Tooting family pancakes. He showed it to Dad and gave him a thumbs-up before filling two big cans of petrol for them. As they walked back, with the white stars reeling overhead and campfires glowing to the left and right, they could hear people singing strange and lovely songs. Dad said, 'You know, I could live like this. We could stay here and run this place as a proper business. We could call it Café Café Bang Bang. We could offer people pleasure flights across the pyramids. We could be the hottest spot in Cairo.'

And just then Jem thought he might be right.

The first ray of sunlight was slicing the horizon when the Tooting family shut up shop and followed Lucy to the feet of the Sphinx. The Sphinx looked even bigger close up. The last few visitors – sitting around their campfire – hardly reached her toenails. Dad asked one of them to take a photograph of the whole family with the Sphinx, but the man had to walk so far away to fit the monument in that they looked like a speck of dirt at the bottom of the picture. There was nothing to do but stand and stare and let that magical sight sink into their memories. Lucy told them the legend of a Sphinx who guarded a road and would not let travellers pass unless they could correctly answer her riddle. If you got it wrong, she would eat you. How the statue had been built four and a half thousand years ago. Or three thousand years ago, depending which theory you believed. How legend had it that Napoleon's soldiers had accidentally broken its nose while they were practising nearby with their cannons. She described what it looked like when it was new, before the wind and sand had chewed it up – how it had the body of a lion and the wings of an eagle.

But Mum wasn't listening. 'Little Harry!' she gasped. 'Where is he? Where is Little Harry?'

The visitors had gone now and so had everyone else. Little Harry was nowhere to be seen.

'Look!' yelled Jem. He had spotted a set of small footprints toddling off into the desert.

They followed Little Harry's footprints as fast and far as they could. But then a morning breeze started up, blowing sand into their faces and smoothing away every print and smudge from the surface of the desert, making it flat and blank. All around there was nothing to see but sand and the blue air wobbling in the heat. It was as though a terrible invisible hand had come along and rubbed Little Harry out.

They looked behind them. They could no longer see the Sphinx, the pyramids, the sightseers or their cars or even the van. It wasn't just Little Harry that had been erased. It was the whole world.

'Little Harry! Little Harry!' they called, but their voices were snatched away in front of their faces.

'We should split up,' said Mum. 'You and Jem go that

way. I'll go this way with Lucy. He can't be far.'

'If we separate we might all vanish,' said Dad. 'We might never find each other again.'

'We have to do something!' said Mum. 'We can't just stand here!' She was feeling headachy and hot. She wanted to run, but she didn't know which way to go.

'Excuse me.' It was a gentle, soothing voice, and it came from just behind them. A woman, dressed all in red, with red hair and red sunglasses, was smiling at them with red lips from under the wide shade of a huge red umbrella.

The woman said calmly, 'Could this be the dear Little Harry you're looking for?'

Holding one of the woman's fingers (her nails were painted red), smiling up at them from the shade, was Little Harry. 'Babies!' yelled Little Harry.

'My baby,' said Mum, sweeping him up in her arms and kissing him. 'Don't ever wander off again. Especially in a desert.'

'Babies!' yelled Little Harry.

'Oh, don't be cross with Little Harry,' said the lady in red. 'It was really all the Nanny's fault.'

'Who's the Nanny?' said Dad.

'I'm the Nanny. Silly Nanny was walking through the desert with a hole in her packet of jelly babies, see?' She passed Dad a paper bag with a few jelly babies in it. 'Do take one,' she said, 'Mr . . . ?'

'Tooting. Don't mind if I do. This is my wife, Julie. You've met Little Harry. This is Lucy and this is Jeremy.'

'Jeremy.' Nanny smiled. 'What a deliciously old-fashioned name.'

Jem winced.

'I seem to have been dropping jelly babies every few yards. Little Harry spotted one, ate it, spotted another, went after it, ate that and followed the jelly-baby trail all the way out here. Didn't you, Little Harry? Still, no harm done, though he's a bit sticky.'

Mum wiped Little Harry's face and said, 'I can't believe I didn't see him wandering off. I'm always so careful with him.'

'It's entirely understandable,' soothed Nanny. 'After all, you were seeing the Sphinx for the very first time. That's quite a distraction. Sometimes all it takes is a moment. Do come under Nanny's umbrella.'

They all shuffled under the umbrella. It's amazing what a difference a bit of cloth on a stick can make. Suddenly they could breathe again. And see. Without the sun blazing in their eyes, it was easy for them to spot the Sphinx, just a few hundred yards away. And the pyramids. And Chitty Chitty Bang Bang. They hadn't gone far at all. They had been tricked by the heat.

'You all look so hot and bothered,' said Nanny. 'Please, have a drink.'

She took a bottle of water from her big red handbag and passed it round. The water was icy cold, which is a bit strange when you think about it. Nobody thought about it just then though. They were all too happy drinking it.

'Say sorry to the lady for eating her jelly babies,' said Dad to Little Harry.

'Oh, they weren't for me.' Nanny smiled. 'I was taking them home to my little charge. It's my morning off. I always do a bit of archaeology on my days off, and I always take a present back to my little one.'

'Archaeology?' said Lucy. 'That's interesting. So which is your favourite Sphinx theory? Three thousand years old or four and a half?'

'Oh, I'm not interested in the Sphinx at all. Or the pyramids. It's automotive archaeology that interests me. Come and see . . .'

She led them to a spot just over the next dune where some men were digging what looked like a set of

old tyres out of the sand and loading them on to the backs of a couple of camels.

'These,' she said, 'are the wheels from an old racing car. My theory is that they fell off during the Timbuktu–Cairo rally of 1922 – one of the greatest motor races of all time. I'm so happy that we've found all four wheels.'

One of the men shouted something excitedly. 'He says,' translated Lucy, 'that he's found a fifth wheel. Maybe it's the spare?' The man was brushing the sand from a big wooden wheel, inlaid with gold and lapis lazuli. Carved crocodiles chased each other through ivory papyrus all around the rim.

'Dinosaurs,' said Little Harry.

'Beautiful,' said Mum.

'That's not the spare tyre, silly,' said Nanny. 'That's just the wheel of some old pharaoh's ceremonial chariot. Leave it in the sand. My racing wheels are much more interesting.'

It turned out that there was something very interesting about the racing wheels. Jem was the first to spot it. 'Dad! Come and look at this.' Dozens of shiny steel spokes radiated from a thick silver hubcap, and engraved in curly letters across the middle of the cap was the word 'Zborowski'.

'What a coincidence!' said Dad. 'Your wheels have got the same name as our engine.'

'*You have a Zborowski engine?*' gasped Nanny. 'Can I see?'

So, while the men with the camels took the Zborowski wheels away, Nanny followed the Tooting family back to Chitty Chitty Bang Bang. 'Isn't that a camper van – a twenty-three-window Samba Bus, the kind beloved by adventurous families?' said Nanny.

'Exactly right,' said Dad. 'You certainly know your stuff.'

'The little boy I look after is crazy about cars. Aren't all little boys? I bet you are too, aren't you, Jeremy? But surely the Zborowski engine wouldn't fit in a camper van? Doesn't the Zborowski engine start with a hand crank? Whoever heard of a hand-cranked camper van?'

'Jem . . .' said Dad.

Jem held up the crank handle for her to see.

'Well, how utterly charming,' she said. 'A crank-started camper van. Does she have a name?'

'Chitty Chitty Bang Bang!' yelled Little Harry.

'Of course,' said Nanny. 'Well good morning, Chitty Chitty . . . Oh! Excuse me!' A car horn seemed to be honking very nearby. 'My phone,' she explained, 'has an automobile theme of course.' She glanced at the screen. 'It's a text from my little boy. He's wondering where I am. I'm a bit late . . .'

Dad was slightly startled to see that her mobile phone was shaped just like a larger-than-average jelly baby. Before he had time to think about this, Mum had offered Nanny a lift. 'It's the least we can do. You saved Little Harry's life.'

'I'm sure you'd have saved it yourselves eventually,' said Nanny. 'But if you insist. I would love to hear the roar of that Zborowski engine.' She climbed into the front passenger seat, fastened her seat belt and said, 'Straight on until we get to the main road.'

'Your mobile phone,' said Dad. 'I think I've seen one like that before.'

'Oh, what a fabulous sound that engine makes. Twelve pistons. Twenty-three litres. A symphony of horsepower.'

Dad was impressed. 'You really do know about cars.'

'I pick up titbits here and there, you know . . .' And Nanny told them the story of Count Zborowski, the man whose name appeared on her wheels and their engine. She told them how he had built a massive car in the 1920s in order to try to break the World Land Speed Record.

'So this is a famous historical engine you have under the bonnet there. If you don't mind my asking, though –' she placed a red-painted fingernail on Dad's cheek and turned his face towards her and continued in a low voice – 'since this is the Zborowski engine, where is the Zborowski Lightning?'

'What's the Zborowski Lightning?' said Dad.

Nanny stared at Dad for a while, then smiled as though she'd solved a puzzle. 'I see,' she said. 'You don't want to talk about it. I'm sorry. I should have guessed. You're right, I'm inexcusably nosy, but you're too nice to say so.'

'I never said that. Did I say that?'

'Not in so many words.'

'No, really. We don't know what it is. What is it?'

'The Lightning is the Zborowski insignia. It goes on the front. A Jaguar has a silver jaguar. A Rolls-Royce has a flying lady. The Zborowski engine had the Zborowski Lightning. It's just a pretty decoration, that's all. People who love cars get fascinated by things like that – like those old-fashioned indicators that were actually little luminous paddles that popped out of the sides of a car, or the 1973 Austin Allegro, which had a square steering wheel. Turn right here.'

ROLLS-ROYCE

JAGUAR

ZBOROWSKI

Dad drove the van on to a dusty road. Ahead of them they could see water and a little bridge leading to an avenue of palm trees. 'Over the bridge,' said Nanny, 'and then straight through the gates . . .'

'Just to go back to the subject of your mobile . . . oh, wow!' said Dad as they drove through the gates.

'Whoa!' said Lucy as the gates closed behind them.

'Goodness!' said Mum as she held Little Harry up to the window.

'You live here?' gasped Jem. 'This is a palace.'

'Welcome,' said Nanny, 'to Château Bateau.'

Graceful white towers and delicate minarets rose from behind a screen of palm trees and fig trees. Through the branches of an orange grove Jem saw water rippling and flickering in the sun. 'Is that a swimming pool?' he said. 'Can we go in?'

'Jem,' said Mum sternly.

'Not at all,' said Nanny. 'You're all welcome to swim for as long as you like.'

'No, no,' said Mum. 'Really you've done so much for us already.'

But Nanny insisted. She said that she was sure the little boy she looked after would love to see their extraordinary camper van and that in the meantime they really must use the pool. She showed them to the changing rooms, which were little log cabins right by the pool. Each one had a pile of fluffy white towels inside. She pointed out a shower hidden under a spreading grapevine.

'Oh! A shower! I haven't had a shower for ages!' sighed Lucy.

'I guessed,' said Nanny with a smile.

'You mean we smell?' Mum was horrified.

'I mean you're on a great adventure. You deserve a little pampering and a rest. You look as if you've been up all night, Mr Tooting. Come on, let's park your van while the others spoil themselves. Jem, maybe you'd like to see the garage too.'

The garage at Château Bateau was not like other

garages. As they drove in through the elegant marble archway, fragrant soapy water poured over their van, washing the desert sands away. The ramp was carpeted with deep spongy material that cleaned and polished the tyres. Perfumed breezes circulated from hidden recesses, blowing away the soapy bubbles and drying the windscreen and the mirrors. Instead of a parking space, each car had a sort of bedroom, with its own door to shut out the rest of the world.

'I think Chitty Chitty Bang Bang will be quite comfortable here in room twenty-three.' Nanny smiled again.

'The word today is *car heaven*,' said Dad.

'Take a peek inside the other rooms – why not?' said Nanny. 'We do have some very nice vehicles here. Go on, pick a door . . .'

Jem opened the door next to Chitty's and gasped. Inside was a vast Rolls-Royce with headlamps like new moons and bodywork that shone with a soft, buttery light.

'Yes,' said Nanny, 'it's made of gold. It belonged to the Maharajah of Jammu and Kashmir. I sort of persuaded him to give it to my little boy.'

'Wait . . . this belongs to a little boy?' said Dad.

'I know. I know. I spoil him. But honestly, if you'd seen his little face. It made him *so* happy.'

'I'd be happy too,' said Jem, 'if my dad bought me a gold-plated Rolls-Royce.'

'It's not gold-plated. It's solid gold. That's just it,

you see. My poor little chap doesn't have a daddy. Or a mummy. All he has is me.'

'Oh, he's an orphan?' said Dad. 'How sad.'

'It's more complicated than that. His parents are very wealthy. They put all their assets in his name for tax purposes, and then . . . well, I can't say any more for legal reasons. Let's just say they're not available. It's just the two of us. Jeremy, don't go too close.'

Jem had wanted to look inside the Rolls-Royce but Nanny pulled him back. 'We didn't want to fit an alarm to such a beautiful old machine,' she explained, 'but we don't want anyone to steal it. So we've had to make special security arrangements. There they are, look . . .'

She pointed a perfect red fingernail at the front tyres. Two thick, sinewy snakes had slid out from under the car and were wriggling towards Jem. One of them reared up. Its hood flashed open and its tongue flicked in and out between its sharp fangs. Jem jumped back.

'King Cobras,' said Nanny. 'They belonged to the maharajah too. He threw them in with the car. Very kind of him. So much more effective than one of those noisy electric alarms.'

'Quick,' said Dad. 'Shut the door.'

Jem slammed the door of the little room just as the snake hurled itself towards him. They heard the dull *thunk* of its body hitting the wood. This narrow escape from the jaws of a deadly snake didn't seem to concern Nanny one bit. She was busy scrolling through the photographs on her jelly-baby phone. 'Look,' she said, 'there's my little chap the day he got the Rolls.'

It was a tiny figure sitting on a chair. His feet didn't come to the end of the cushion and his shoulders did not come up to the armrests.

'He's really tiny,' said Jem.

'He's tiny, but his heart is huge. Can you see? A gold Rolls-Royce is a small price to pay for a smile like that, don't you think?'

'I remember Tiny Jack,' said Dad suddenly. 'He rang me. He tried to buy Chitty Chitty Bang Bang off me.'

'Oh, the naughty boy,' tutted Nanny, snapping her phone shut. 'He knows he's not supposed to use the phone without permission. How did he know your number?'

'He didn't. I was on a French television programme called *Car Stupide* . . .'

'Oh, he does love that programme. Were you really on it? He'll be so excited to talk to you about it. I can't wait for you to meet him . . .'

Something about all this was making Dad feel uncomfortable. Tiny Jack wanted Chitty Chitty Bang Bang. Now Chitty Chitty Bang Bang was in Tiny Jack's house. But Tiny Jack was just a little boy with a nanny to look after him . . .

Dad was still trying to figure all this out when he was distracted by the swimming pool. To be fair, anyone would be distracted by the swimming pool at Château Bateau. It wasn't just the cool clear water or the little island in the middle with big jugs of icy lemonade and blackcurrant juice. It wasn't just the lovely little waterfall of warm water that splashed and bubbled in the shallow end. It wasn't even the big inflatable lobster that you could climb on and paddle like a boat. Or the slide that spun you through a spiral of vines and creepers before it chucked you in the deep end. No, the best thing about the pool was the floor. It was not made of tiles or stone slabs. It was sand with urchins and purple sea anemones. Little silver fishes chased each other in and out, tickling your feet as they sped by.

'Come in!' yelled Mum, bobbing about by the waterfall. 'It's not a swimming pool, it's a centrally heated rock pool.'

'Can we stay here for a while?' said Lucy, from somewhere high up on the inflatable lobster's back. 'Like maybe the rest of our lives.'

'I,' said Dad, as he slid into the water, 'could definitely live like this.'

All those little niggling worries he had about jelly-baby phones and tiny-boy car dealers? They all popped like bubbles.

Later that day, Lucy and Jem were still in the pool. Mum and Dad were dozing on sunloungers.

Nanny appeared on the edge of the diving board, in her smart red shoes, her own reflection staring up at her. Jem could see the reflection of her reflection reflected in her big red sunglasses.

'I've had an idea,' she said. 'Mummy and Daddy Tooting have driven their lucky little children halfway around the world. Isn't it time that they had a night off? Why don't you both go out tonight? Cairo is so exciting. You could leave the children here with me. After all, I am a highly trained professional nanny.'

'Oh, we couldn't,' Mum said. 'Really, you've done enough for us already. You saved Little Harry's life. You let us have a shower. You are too kind.'

'Nonsense, Mrs Tooting,' said Nanny, 'you'd be doing me a favour. My little charge sees so few other children. He'd love to play with Lucy and Jeremy and Little

Harry –' she glanced at the children – 'and I'm sure they'd enjoy that too.'

'We'd love it,' said Lucy, sliding into the water from the top of the inflatable lobster.

'Definitely,' said Jem.

'Hide and seek!' shouted Little Harry.

'We sleep in Chitty,' said Mum. 'If Tom and I are out late, that means the children have to stay up late. After the day we've had . . .'

'I did think of that,' said Nanny, 'and I have a solution. Come and see . . .'

Dad and Mum followed Nanny through the palm trees to the gravel drive at the front of the house. This was the first time they'd seen the house properly. The

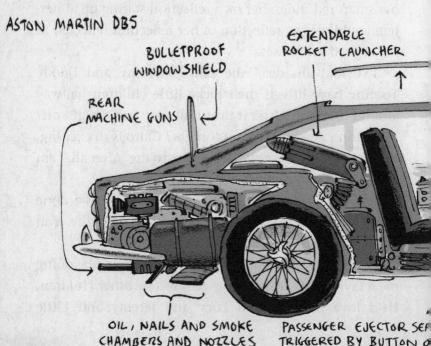

ASTON MARTIN DB5

BULLETPROOF WINDOWSHIELD

EXTENDABLE ROCKET LAUNCHER

REAR MACHINE GUNS

OIL, NAILS AND SMOKE CHAMBERS AND NOZZLES

PASSENGER EJECTOR SEA TRIGGERED BY BUTTON O FLIP-UP GEAR KNOB flight of steps that ran down from the front door like a marble waterfall, the fountain splashing in the drive and the carp flashing in the fountain, the cloisters that spread on each side behind their groves of slender white pillars – Dad didn't notice any of this. Because Dad was staring at the car in the drive. It was sleek and small and silver and so streamlined that it looked like it was speeding even though it was standing still.

'It's an Aston Martin,' said Nanny.

'Aston Martin DB5,' sighed Dad. 'I used to dream about this car.'

'I know it's very fast and sporty, but it's also got some excellent safety features. For instance –' she leaned inside and flipped a switch, and a metal panel rose slowly out of

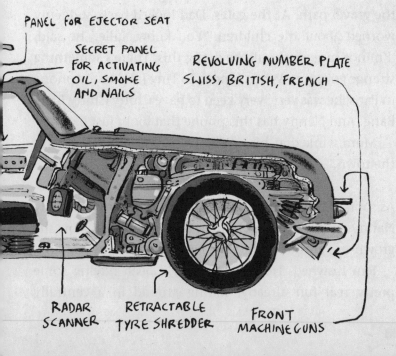

PANEL FOR EJECTOR SEAT

SECRET PANEL
FOR ACTIVATING
OIL, SMOKE
AND NAILS

REVOLVING NUMBER PLATE
SWISS, BRITISH, FRENCH

RADAR
SCANNER

RETRACTABLE
TYRE SHREDDER

FRONT
MACHINE GUNS

the rear – 'adjustable bulletproof armour.'

'That could be useful,' said Dad.

'This button is for the ejector seat, just in case. And there are two guns housed under the front headlights. You probably won't need them . . .'

'Probably not. We were thinking of just going to get a pizza or something, weren't we?'

'Then I won't bother explaining the smokescreen or the rocket launcher. Just enjoy the drive . . .'

Dad climbed into the car in a happy daze. Then Mum made him climb out again and sit in the passenger seat.

'But I really want to drive it!' he complained.

'Well you can't. Look at yourself. You're much too happy to drive. You're practically floating. I'll drive.'

So she did. Once around the fountain and off down the gravel path. At the gates, Dad looked back, suddenly worried about the children. 'You know, Julie,' he said, 'I'm not sure we should be doing this. There's something strange going on. When I spoke to Tiny Jack on the phone in Paris, he was very, very keen to have Chitty Chitty Bang Bang. And Nanny has this phone that looks just like—'

Mum winked at him. 'You worry too much. Let's hit the town.'

As soon as the Aston Martin slipped out through the gate Nanny returned to the children and said, 'Right. Now the grown-ups are out of the way, let's all have some real fun.'

Jem frowned. He thought they'd been having some pretty real fun already, lolling around in a centrally heated rock pool, drinking lemonade, while fish nibbled their toes. But then Nanny said, 'To begin with, would you mind if I called you Jem instead of Jeremy?'

'No. Oh. No, I'd like that.'

'I thought so. I have no idea why grown-ups like those long curly old names.' As she said this, she bent down and pressed a hidden button and suddenly all the water in the pool was a churning riot of bubbles.

'Swim!' shouted Little Harry and jumped right in, not realizing he couldn't swim.

Jem had to rescue him. 'This is nice,' he said, 'but it must be bad for the fish.'

'The way I see it,' said Nanny, 'if you like it, then the fish probably like it too.'

'Good point,' said Lucy.

'Enjoy it now, and maybe in a little while Tiny Jack will come and play.'

So Lucy tried to swim to the bottom while the bubbles streamed into her face, pushing her up again. She flipped over on her back and the bubbles propelled her across the pool like a rocket. It was then that she came to the conclusion that this was so much fun that everything that had happened before was only a fraction of fun. This was complete fun. Jem and Little Harry agreed.

When the sun sank lower in the sky and they grew chilly Nanny lit a little bonfire at the side of the pool and gave them sausages and showed them how to cook them in the flames, using toasting forks. Afterwards she did the same with marshmallows.

'Having fun?' She smiled.

'So much fun,' said Jem. 'But what about Tiny Jack? You said he might like to come and play.'

'Silly me! I was having such a nice time,' said Nanny, 'I forgot all about him. What a bad Nanny! I'll go and ask him if he'd like a game of Monopoly. Or Snakes and Ladders.'

'Does he only like old-fashioned games?' said Jem, feeling a stab of disappointment for the first time since entering Château Bateau.

'Old-fashioned?'

'It's just . . . a house like this – I thought he'd have PlayStations and Xboxes and a Wii. I thought he'd want to play *Mario Kart*.'

'*Mario Kart*? What's *Mario Kart*?'

'It's a game – a racing-car game. We each have a steering wheel and you choose a car from all kinds of different designs . . .'

'Wait. Are you talking about a computer game?' said Nanny. 'Because I never let Tiny Jack play with computer games. I think they're bad for children. I like him to play real games. If that's old-fashioned, call me old-fashioned.'

'Well . . .' said Jem, 'I just thought . . .' He felt a bit guilty. He didn't want to appear ungrateful when they were having such a good time.

Nanny didn't seem to notice. She carried on. 'So if he wants to play a motor-racing game, for instance, I let him use a real car. On a real race track.'

It took a moment for this to sink into Jem's and Lucy's brains.

'So . . . if we wanted to play a motor-racing game right now . . . ?'

'Of course. Let's go and see what we've got in the Toy Box.'

The Château Bateau Toy Box was a building the size of a small church stuck on one side of the château itself. The floor was paved with huge versions of board games. There was a Monopoly board that you could walk around. It had got playing pieces big enough to sit in and pedal, and a massive oak trunk full of money.

'Excuse me, Nanny,' said Lucy, 'isn't this real money?'

'Yes of course. Now, this is one of Tiny Jack's favourites.'

'It's just squares with numbers on . . .'

'Snakes and ladders!' yelled Little Harry.

'Clever boy, Little Harry,' said Nanny. 'The ladders are over there . . .' She pointed to a copse of stepladders propped up in the corner. 'And there are the snakes.' She waved her red-painted nails towards a tank of pythons, twisting around each other, sliding up and down the glass.

'Snakes and ladders with real snakes,' said Lucy. 'Now *that* is stylish.'

'Lego,' said Nanny, pointing to what looked like a building site strewn with mounds of the stuff – hods and trucks and wheelbarrows full of the coloured bricks. There was a half-built Lego house that would easily sleep a family of four, and a helicopter that looked like it might really fly, but much as he loved Lego, Jem looked at Nanny when she said, 'We also have racing cars. Jem, you love to play with racing cars, don't you?'

Jem didn't want to be rude, but the last racing cars he'd seen were the ones that Dad had installed in his bedroom. Why couldn't people just be happy with nice, safe, tidy computer versions that didn't whizz past you or send electric sparks up your nose?

'We've got a blue one and a red one,' said Nanny.

Just like Dad's, thought Jem.

'They're in here . . .' She led them into a bright, airy room and there were the cars. They were exactly like Dad's ones. The only difference was that Dad's were little plastic models and these were real racing cars.

'Who's going to be red and who's going to be blue?' asked Nanny.

'Me red!' shouted Little Harry and toddled off towards the blue car.

'No, no, Harry, you're too little,' said Lucy, picking him up. 'So are we,' she added quickly. 'We can't drive.'

'I actually can,' said Jem. 'I honestly think I can. Really.' He couldn't bear the idea of not getting into one of those racing cars.

'Yes, but we're not allowed to drive. We don't have licences.'

Nanny shrugged. 'Neither does Tiny Jack.'

'Of course not,' said Jem. 'He's too little.'

'Exactly.' Nanny pointed a remote-control device at the door. It flashed and beeped and rose to reveal a black racing track, smooth as satin, snaking off through the gardens of Château Bateau.

'What if we crash?' said Lucy.

'You almost certainly will. It's half the fun,' said Nanny, smiling. 'Don't worry about the cars – they're pretty indestructible.'

'I was worrying about us.'

'I'm not worried,' said Jem, and he jumped into the seat of the red car (everyone knows red is fastest). The moment he got in, the arms of the seat closed around him and held him tight. There was a faint whirring noise as a mechanical arm hoisted a padded helmet on to his head. It did all feel very safe.

'Me driving!' yelled Little Harry.

'No, Little Harry,' said Lucy, climbing into the blue car. 'It's not safe. You stay with Nanny.'

'Oh, but he will be driving,' said Nanny, as the seat folded its arms around Lucy. 'They're remote-controlled cars.' She passed Little Harry a console with a little driving wheel on it just like the ones Dad had used for the toy cars. Little Harry pressed the button gleefully and Jem's car lurched forward at terrifying speed, then stopped suddenly.

Nanny was in charge of the blue car. Clearly she'd spent many happy hours over the years playing with remote-control cars and now it slid smoothly round the track with Lucy in the driver's seat, easing into bends and hurtling down the straights.

Little Harry on the other hand had never played with remote-control cars before. I don't know if you've ever ridden in a full-sized turbo-charged racing car operated by an inexperienced three-year-old, but it's not an experience you'd ever forget. Jem's car spun and skidded round the first bend, then pootled very slowly down the straight bit before powerfully accelerating into a terrifying chicane. Jem was buffeted from side to side as the car fishtailed from left to right. His brain was so pulverized that he almost forgot to scream with terror as the car hurtled towards a huge ramp that ended in mid-air. Right on the brink of the drop, the car screeched to a halt. Then very, very slowly it slid backwards down the ramp. Phew! thought Jem. Then, without any warning, the car raced up the ramp again, hit the end and rocketed into the air. Jem screwed up his eyes and heard the wind whistling past his ears. Then the car thumped

down on the other side. A second later, Lucy's car landed deftly next to his and sped quietly on its way – already on its second lap.

After the first, terrifying circuit, Little Harry began to get the hang of the controls and Jem began to enjoy the sound of the engine growling like a box of angry bears, the sunset washing over the broad glossy bonnet, the fragrance of the wind that blew in his face.

The orange-scented sunset turned to moonlight and Jem noticed that he hadn't seen Lucy's car for a couple of laps. The stars came out. The air grew chill. Still Jem was going round and round the race track all on his own. 'Hello?' he called. 'Hello? Would someone stop the car please?'

No one answered.

No sound but the growl and squeal of the car as it sashayed through bends and leaped over the ravine again and again, faster and faster with each lap.

'Hello?' called Jem. 'Excuse me!' as he thundered into a steep bend, banking right at the tip of the track. 'Excuse . . . oh!' The engine had stopped dead. The car slithered down from the top of the track and rolled over twice on to the verge, ending up on its back.

When Jem crawled free the first thing he saw was Lucy looking down at him with Little Harry in her arms. Nanny put her finger to her lips, telling Jem to shush, then pointed at Little Harry. 'Fast asleep,' she whispered. 'He dropped off right on top of the remote control. We tried to prise it out from underneath him or sneak it out of his hands but he kept waking up and objecting.'

'I've got him now.' Lucy smiled. 'Let's put him to bed. Come on, Jem. Let's go and open up Chitty.'

'No,' said Nanny. 'No sleeping in Chitty tonight. Tonight you'll sleep in Proper Beds.'

Proper Beds.

Until Nanny said those words, Jem and Lucy had been perfectly comfortable sleeping in Chitty Chitty Bang Bang. Yes, it was a bit cramped. Yes, the beds were really only shelves with thin mattresses on. But it was cosy and warm and nice to lie there, chatting while the stars popped out.

The phrase 'Proper Beds' made them remember what it was like to have space to roll over in the night, to stretch out, to read under the duvet. They were so tired by then that Proper Beds seemed even more exciting than real racing cars.

Bats were flitting in and out of the pillars as they

followed Nanny along the moonlit cloister, up the broad white steps, and into the house itself. The floor of the entrance hall was tiled black and white squares – like the chequered flag in motor racing. Dangling from the ceiling was an enormous chandelier made of hundreds of little cardboard pine trees – like the air fresheners you see in cars. Standing on the floor was a massive silver statue of St Christopher, the Patron Saint of Motorists. At his feet was a big model of a dog made of some sort of furry material. As Nanny led the children past, the dog's head nodded slowly up and down. All the lamps looked like various kinds of car headlights, and the banisters were huge chrome bumpers. 'Tiny Jack really does like cars,' said Jem.

Nanny smiled. 'He really does.'

'We never played with him,' said a sleepy Lucy.

'Maybe tomorrow,' said Nanny.

All the way up the stairs were framed photographs of Tiny Jack. There was one of him eating a Toblerone. Next to him the chocolate bar looked as big as a ladder.

'He really is small,' said Lucy.

'He really is.' Nanny smiled again, as though being small was a great achievement. 'Now it's time for bed.'

She opened a door that was unusual for a bedroom door – yellow, made of metal, with a shiny handle and a little window – but would have looked perfectly normal on a New York taxicab. The room inside though looked nothing like the inside of a car. Well . . . the picture window did have windscreen wipers and the mirror did

look like a big rear-view mirror, but apart from that it just looked like a very comfortable bedroom. A log fire blazed merrily in the grate, and by its warm, flickering light the children saw three big beds made up in crisp white linen. Beside each bed was a little table and on each table was a glass of milk, a torch, and a choice of books. On each pillow was a neatly folded pair of cotton pyjamas. Just looking at those pyjamas made you feel dreamy and contented. The wall and ceiling around Lucy's bed were painted matt black. Lucy clapped her hands and said, 'How did you know?'

Nanny didn't answer. She quickly and quietly turned down one of the duvets so that Lucy could slip Little Harry underneath without waking him. Then she wished them pleasant dreams and tiptoed out.

It was the best night's sleep Lucy had ever had. Every now and then she woke in the night, but only just enough for her to have that delicious feeling you get when you realize it's still not morning and you can go back to sleep.

Jem, on the other hand, didn't sleep a wink. At first it was because he was so excited. He wanted to tell Dad all about driving the racing cars. Then he didn't sleep because he was thinking, why aren't they back yet? And why are there so many snakes in this place? And why didn't we ever see Tiny Jack?

The sun stole into the room. Lucy stretched and yawned. Jem said, 'Mum and Dad aren't back.'

'How do you know? They're probably by the pool having breakfast right now.'

'I think I would have heard the muscular but musical engine of an Aston Martin DB5 pulling up, don't you?'

'So what if they're not back yet? We're not in any hurry to leave, are we, Little Harry?' He had climbed into her bed at some point in the night. 'We're going for another big swim . . .' She started to get the swimming things together.

'Nanny kept saying that Tiny Jack would be thrilled to meet us but did he come and meet us? Did we even see him?'

'She said he was having a nap.'

'A nap? Hibernation, more like. And why is she just called Nanny?'

'Because she's just the nanny. I think that's quite cool actually.'

'The nanny of the invisible hibernating boy. And she never takes her sunglasses off. Even at night.'

'Also quite cool.'

'OK. Well, this last thing is definitely worrying.'

'What?'

'Cairo has gone.'

'What does that mean, "Cairo has gone"?'

'Cairo was there and now it's not there. Look out of the window . . .'

Cairo is sometimes called the City of a Thousand Minarets – because it has so many beautiful mosques, all with towers and spires and domes and minarets. But looking out of the bedroom window that morning, Lucy and Little Harry saw not a thousand minarets but none. Cairo is home to over six million people. Lucy, Little Harry and Jem looked through that window as hard as they could. They saw . . . not six million people – but no people. None. Not one.

The beautiful gardens of Château Bateau and the lovely figure-of-eight racetrack where they'd driven the racing cars – they were all still there. Beyond the garden gate – nothing but water as far as the horizon.

'We seem,' said Lucy, pushing open the window, 'to be at sea.'

Now that there were seagulls squawking around their heads and blue waves rolling all around them and a salty breeze blowing through their hair, something was obvious that had not been obvious the night before. Château Bateau was not a house. Château Bateau was a boat.

'The clue was in the name, I suppose,' said Lucy.

The beautiful villa, the gardens, the racetrack, these were all nothing but the top deck. Château Bateau was a boat, and it had set sail with the children on board. And their parents . . . not on board.

'Judging from wind direction and the angle of the sun, and taking into consideration the maximum amount of time that we could possibly have been on the high seas without actually noticing, I would say we're in the Arabian Sea, heading south towards Madagascar.'

'I want my Mummy!' yelled Little Harry.

'I think we need to ask Nanny a few questions,' said Lucy.

'What a beautiful morning,' said Nanny when they found her by the pool. 'Look, Nanny's made you a lovely breakfast.'

'Nanny,' said Lucy, 'this is a boat.'

'Of course it is – that's why it's called Château Bateau. Mr Fink got it for Tiny Jack on his birthday.'

'Who's Mr Fink?'

'Tiny Jack's father of course – you must have heard of him. He was quite famous. Man-Mountain Fink? Poor Tiny Jack always feels that he is not really the kind of son that Man-Mountain expected.'

They hadn't heard of him – and besides, they were more interested in their own parents than in Tiny Jack's.

'Isn't this just the most fun ever?' Nanny smiled. 'We've run away to sea. Don't all children secretly yearn to run away to sea?'

'I want my mummy!' bawled Little Harry.

'Let's all have tea and toast and marmalade in the shade,' said Nanny. 'And look, Nanny's made some eggs and bacon – your favourites.' The table was spread with a fresh gingham cloth and a vase of flowers, a toast rack full of toast, a hotplate laden with bacon rashers and scrambled eggs, a jug of orange juice, all in the shade of . . .

It was then that Jem noticed what was making the shade. A massive stone face was staring out across the dunes from behind the orange blossom.

'Nanny,' he said, 'isn't that the Sphinx?'

'Good heavens!' said Nanny. 'So it is.'

'But what is the Sphinx doing here?'

'That little scamp Tiny Jack must have stolen it. He is a good boy, but he can be very light-fingered.'

'*Light-fingered*? The Sphinx . . . Nanny, he can't have stolen the Sphinx. The Sphinx has been there for four and a half thousand years. Or three thousand, depending which theory you believe.'

'So definitely time for a change then,' said Nanny. 'Tiny Jack's not all bad.'

'I want my mummy!' yelled Little Harry.

'He really does want his mummy,' said Jem.

'Don't worry about Mummy and Daddy. They are having a wonderful time cruising around in a fabulous car.'

'We can't just leave them behind. They're our mum and dad.'

Nanny looked puzzled. 'But you said it would be more fun without them.'

'I didn't say that,' said Jem. He looked at Lucy. 'Did you say that?'

'I don't think so. No.'

'You said that they would never have let you drive.'

'Yes . . . but . . .'

'He wouldn't let you drive Chitty Chitty Bang Bang even though you practically built her.'

'That's true,' said Jem.

'He's mean,' said Nanny.

'I want my mummy! I want my mummy!'

'He's not mean. He's just safety-conscious. Please take us back now.'

'Why, certainly.' Nanny smiled. 'We'll go back right away.'

'Thank you.'

'Of course what with currents, prevailing winds, shipping lanes and all that nonsense, a vessel this size can't just do a three-point turn. We have to go all the way around the coast of Africa to get back to where we started. What fun! Haven't you always dreamed of doing something like this? We're pirates!'

'But . . .' said Jem.

'Nanny! Where's my nanny?'

A whiny voice was screaming somewhere nearby.

'I want my nanny. Where is my nanny? Why is she ignoring me?'

The children looked round. Finally they were going to meet Tiny Jack. But the sound was coming from a little plastic bluebird with an aerial, sitting on the breakfast table.

'Excuse me,' said Nanny, switching it off. 'The alarm. That means I'm wanted . . . and just as I was about to feed the fish.' She lifted up her sunglasses and possibly winked at them. I say possibly, because her eyes were hard to see. They were very tiny with long, tangled lashes caked in mascara. Against the deathly white of her face they looked like two squashed spiders on top of a wedding cake. 'Enjoy your breakfast and your swim,' she said, and hurried off into the house.

'Swim!' said Little Harry, toddling towards the pool.

'No!' yelled Lucy, pulling him back and hoisting him into her arms. 'We have to get out of here. Nanny just tried to kill us.'

'What?'

'The fish in the pool, the little silver ones – notice anything about them yesterday?'

'They were quite tickly.'

'Piranhas. Capable of stripping every ounce of flesh from a human body in thirty seconds.'

'But we were swimming with them.'

'Piranhas will only attack you if they're hungry. Yesterday they weren't hungry. Today, she's just told us, she hasn't fed them.'

'How did you know they weren't hungry yesterday?'

'They didn't look hungry. And anyway, I thought, well,

if you're going to die young then being stripped to the skeleton by a shoal of starving piranhas in the grounds of a mysterious château is a pretty impressive way to go.'

'But I don't want to die young.'

'If we don't get out of here,' said Lucy, 'that's exactly what's going to happen.'

'I suppose she might have forgotten that they're man-eating fish.'

Lucy picked up some bacon from the hotplate and tossed it into the pool. Immediately the water churned and boiled as the ravenous piranhas swarmed in a frenzy around the meat. 'That might have been us,' said Lucy. 'We should get out of here. But how?'

'Well,' said Jem, 'we do just happen to have the greatest getaway vehicle in the history of the world . . .'

Lucy grabbed Little Harry and followed Jem to the garage, where he quickly found car bedroom number 23. He yanked open the door and they all hurried inside. They stared in horror.

Chitty Chitty Bang Bang was in there.

In pieces.

Someone had taken her apart.

The mighty engine sat in the middle

of the room, but the wheels, the axles, the
doors, the wings, the roof, the seats had all
been pulled off and piled up in corners.

'She's dead,' gasped Lucy. 'Dead, dead, dead.'

'Chitty Chitty no go,' sighed Little Harry.

'What are we going to do?' asked Lucy.

'I want my mummy,' said Little Harry.

For a long moment, Jem said nothing. He was
looking around the room, ticking things off in his head,
remembering the days when he had first helped Dad put
this van together. 'It's all right,' he said. 'It's going to be
all right. She's all here. She's just not in the right order.
We can fix her. Lucy, pass me that spanner.'

'You can't build a whole van,' said Lucy.

'Done it before,' said Jem. 'Now pass that wrench there.'
She passed the wrench.

'A van like Chitty,' said Jem, 'is not just a heap of
components. You can take her apart. You can take bits away.
But somehow she'll still be Chitty.'

'That's what Dad said when we first got her.'

'Exactly.'

'And it took him two months to put her together. Do we want to spend two months piranha-dodging?'

'It'll be different this time. The most important part of Chitty is here, in my head.'

'How come? Did you swallow it or something?'

'Help me put this wing back on to the frame here.' What was in Jem's head was the memory of those summer days helping his dad piece the van together. If you've solved a puzzle once, you can always solve it again more quickly. More than that, this time Jem knew that Chitty would help him. That the van wanted to be herself again.

'Why would Nanny do a thing like this?' said Lucy, lifting the wing panel into place.

'To stop us escaping, of course. Can you get this jack underneath? . . . That's it.'

'No, she doesn't care about us. She was going to feed us to the piranhas. It's all about the van. She wants Chitty. Or Tiny Jack does. But why? When he's got so many amazing cars already.'

'Chitty's amazing too,' said Jem. 'And she's going to be amazing again. Headlights, please.'

Soon Chitty Chitty Bang Bang began to look herself again. Because Dad and Jem had done such a good job the first time – every screw was clean and oiled, every bolt and nut perfectly aligned – that now she was slotting together quite easily. They were just beginning to feel optimistic when a voice behind them said,

'It doesn't look anything like it looked in the pictures. It's just a scruffy old camper van . . .'

It was the voice of Tiny Jack. They spun round and stared at the door, expecting him to walk in at any second.

'And I took it completely apart and I still couldn't find the Zborowoski Lightning. I'm disappointed. I'm very disappointed.'

The door didn't open. The voice was coming from somewhere in the room. In fact it was coming from Little Harry's hand. He was holding a plastic bluebird with an aerial. Nanny's alarm. It had an on–off switch and the words 'A-Little-Bird-Told-Me Baby Monitor' written across its belly. Nanny must have left it on the breakfast table and Little Harry had brought it with him. They could hear every word that Tiny Jack and Nanny were saying to each other. As they carried on putting Chitty Chitty Bang Bang back together, they listened . . .

'I'm sorry you're disappointed, Tiny Jack. The Lord knows I try my best but it seems to me you're always disappointed. You were even disappointed when I got you those racing cars.'

'Nanny, what I want is a getaway car. My racing cars are fast but they've got no luggage space. I ask you, what's the use of a getaway car with no luggage space? When we did that bank in Mexico, what happened? We were in and out in no time but we had to leave all the money in bags on the pavement.'

'What about the lovely golden Rolls-Royce? It's so shiny that it doesn't show up on security cameras. It's like the invisible car. Most super-criminals would have thought that was very useful. They would have said, "Thank you, Nanny."'

'I did say thank you. I love that car but it's very heavy on petrol. When we did that chocolate shop in Calais we spent more getting there than we got from the robbery. We have to think about the economics of these things.'

'I got you an Aston Martin DB5. Everyone wants one of those. You've actually got one. It's got an ejector seat, secret guns, central locking. What more could you want?'

'It's a mean machine, but you have to admit it has a bad history. That spy who drove it before, he made so many enemies that any time we take it anywhere people recognize it and start shooting at us.'

Jem stared at Lucy in horror.

Lucy clutched Little Harry. She thought of their parents driving round in that very car, being shot at wherever they went. She was only half listening to Tiny Jack now.

Jem was listening fully. Tiny Jack's lack of appreciation of her getaway-car buying ability was making Nanny cross . . .

'You are a very ungrateful boy, Tiny Jack. Most little boys would think themselves lucky if they owned a huge boat disguised as an island with its own helicopter and a pool full of piranhas. They wouldn't even want a getaway car as well.'

'You're always going on about how lucky I am to have Château Bateau, but honestly, have you ever tried to park it? It's a nightmare. Plus it means I can only steal things from coastal areas.'

'You stole the Sphinx.'

'Stealing the Sphinx was fun, but it doesn't put Weetabix on the table. I need a proper getaway car. My dear old dad always said, Tiny, the ultimate getaway car is Chitty Chitty Bang Bang. You get that and you're set for life.'

Once again Lucy and Jem stopped working. 'How could Tiny Jack's dad have known that our camper van was called Chitty Chitty Bang Bang?' said Lucy. 'We only thought of the name when we fell off the Eiffel Tower.'

'Did we think of it though?' said Jem slowly. 'Or did we hear it? Wasn't that the noise Chitty was making? The truth is, she came up with her own name.'

Nanny and Tiny Jack were still bickering . . .

'Chitty Chitty Bang Bang! I got you Chitty Chitty Bang Bang. And what did you do with it? You took it to pieces and left a big mess in the garage. Who's going to tidy that up? Hmm?'

'I was looking for the Lightning. The thing's no use without the Lightning, is it?'

'The Lightning again,' muttered Jem. 'They keep going on about this Lightning thing. What d'you think it is?'

'We can't think about that now,' said Lucy. 'Any minute, Nanny is going to notice that the fish didn't eat us.'

'We don't need to worry about Nanny. Or Tiny Jack,' said Jem. 'Look . . .'

There was Chitty Chitty Bang Bang, completely back in one piece. Jem had even hung the little silver aeroplane from the rear-view mirror, as an ornament. Lucy pulled open the garage door and jumped into the van with Little Harry. Jem turned the crank handle.

Nothing happened.

Not a cough, not a sneeze.

'You've put her together wrong. You've left the batteries out or something.'

'No. I don't think so.'

'Then why doesn't it start? Stupid car.'

'Chitty is not stupid. If she doesn't start, there must be a reason. I just need to think . . .'

'Nanny's coming now. She'll be here any minute . . .'

'I need time to think.'

'OK,' said Lucy. 'Listen – me and Little Harry will go and distract her.'

'Distract her? How can you distract a woman who . . .'

They were already gone.

Lucy and Little Harry watched from behind a palm tree as Nanny strolled over to the swimming pool. They saw her lift her red sunglasses and stare into the water with her little spidery eyes.

'Fishieeees,' she cooed. 'Anybody feed you today?'

Cautiously she put her fingers into the water. Straightaway the water boiled as frenzied fish thrashed around her. She pulled her hand out and held it up. Blood was spurting from a red-taloned fingertip.

'Yuk,' said Little Harry.

The really surprising thing was that Nanny didn't seem to mind. She didn't yelp or try to bandage it. She just carried on chatting to the fish while blood dripped around the pool. 'You haven't been fed, have you? You haven't eaten even one little child. Good. That's good. Because Tiny Jack wants those children alive.'

Lucy picked up Little Harry and strolled out of the cover of the palm trees with a big smile on her face. 'Did you find Tiny Jack? Oh, what happened to your finger?'

'There you are. What are you doing? And where is your brother?'

'We were wondering, Nanny, if Tiny Jack would like to play a game today?'

'I think he definitely would,' said Nanny. 'How about Snakes and Ladders?'

Remembering the board with the real snakes, Lucy shook her head. 'Can't,' she said. 'Little Harry is allergic.'

'What about "What's the time, Mr Wolf?" Do you know that one? It's one of Tiny Jack's favourites.'

As she said this, Lucy heard quite distinctly the lonesome howl of a hungry timber wolf from somewhere on the lower deck. 'Does "What's the Time, Mr Wolf?" involve real wolves?' she asked.

'So much more fun that way,' said Nanny.

Lucy had to think of a way of distracting Nanny that didn't involve being eaten alive. 'I've got a better idea,' she said, desperately trying to think of a game that Tiny Jack might want to play.

'What's that?'

'It's called Hot and Cold. Jem goes and hides something, and you and Tiny Jack have to find it. As you go looking, you're allowed to ask if you're getting hotter or colder.'

Nanny didn't seem convinced.

'What is Jem going to hide?'

This was Lucy's stroke of genius. She said, 'Oh, nothing special. A thing that fell off our van. I think it's called the Lightning.'

We may not know what it is, thought Lucy, but we know you want it.

Nanny looked as if an electric current had shot through her. Although she tried to speak calmly, her whole body seemed to light up with excitement.

'Well, that sounds like a nice idea,' she said, flashing Lucy a mega-kilowatt smile. 'I'll just call Tiny Jack on his mobile and tell him to get down here.'

'No!' said Lucy. 'He's not to move yet. You've got to close your eyes and count to a hundred. Tiny Jack's got to do the same. If you peep, we can't play. We'll just throw the Lightning over the side. That's the rules.'

'Oh, don't do that. I'll call him and tell him.' She called Tiny Jack on her jelly-baby phone.

'Make sure his eyes are closed,' said Lucy. 'We'll come and check.'

'Make sure your eyes are closed. She'll check. She means it,' said Nanny, after she had explained the game to Tiny Jack. Then she covered her own red sunglasses with her long, red-nailed fingers and started to count.

Lucy and Little Harry ran back into the house. If things went to plan, Nanny and Tiny Jack would still be searching while the children made their getaway. As Lucy passed a big doorway she heard a voice quietly muttering, '. . . thirty-six, thirty-seven, thirty-eight . . .' She stopped. She listened. Tiny Jack was behind that big, walnut door. Lucy was suddenly overwhelmed by the desire to see what he looked like. All she had to do was stick her head around the door. She tiptoed closer and peeked inside.

'. . . forty-one, forty-two . . .'

There was no one there. But she could hear Tiny Jack's voice. From behind a second door. Should she walk in and look behind that too? She shushed Little Harry and took a step forward. Then she froze.

There was something in the outer room. A chair. A massive chair. The biggest chair Lucy had ever seen. A chair whose seat was the size of a double bed, whose legs were twelve feet high. Mounted on the wall opposite the chair was a plasma screen with a webcam. Why would anyone need a chair this big, and why would you put a camera facing it?

Lucy realized in a flash: if you sat on a chair this big and had your photograph taken, or filmed yourself, the chair would make you look tiny. Even if you weren't. Even if you were man-sized. Or bigger. In the photographs Tiny Jack's feet came almost to the end of the cushion and his shoulders almost up to the armrests. Tiny Jack must be absolutely huge.

'. . . seventy-eight, seventy-nine . . .' came the voice behind the door.

Lucy stared at the door in terror. In twenty-one seconds' time this giant would come looking for her with his armies of wolves and snakes. She picked up Little Harry, but before she left, she saw one really useful thing – the other piece of the baby monitor plugged into the wall. She grabbed it and ran out through the house. On her way she stopped to plug the speaker end of the monitor into a wall socket behind a cupboard. She took the listening end away with her.

While Lucy was organizing her genius distraction up on deck, Jem was doing his genius car maintenance in the garage. He began by thinking the situation through.

What would Dad do? Chitty wouldn't start. It wasn't a mechanical problem. He had put all the parts in the right place. He'd put everything exactly as it was. Maybe the battery was flat? No, the fabulous headlights were still working. Chitty was not stupid. When she didn't start in Paris, it was for a reason. There had to be a reason now too. In Paris she had wanted her headlights . . .

Maybe she wanted something here.

Lucy burst in carrying Little Harry. 'I think we've got about a minute to get out of here,' she said. 'We also have another problem. Tiny Jack is not tiny.'

'Lucy,' said Jem, 'why did we go to Paris?'

'Because Mum wanted to.'

'I don't think so. It was Chitty who wanted to go to Paris. Why did we go to Cairo?'

'To see the pyramids. It was my idea.'

'What if it wasn't your idea? What if it was Chitty's?'

'Camper vans don't have ideas.'

'Camper vans don't have wings. But Chitty does.'

'So she wanted to be nice to us.'

'I don't think Chitty is interested in us at all. I think she's only interested in Chitty. She landed on top of the Eiffel Tower right next to her old headlights. Why would she land in the desert?'

'Wheels!' yelled Little Harry.

'Shh, Little Harry, we're trying to think,' said Lucy.

'Wheels!'

'Wheels?' said Jem. 'Of course! Remember? Nanny found those Zborowski wheels. They must be Chitty's original wheels. She wants her old wheels back just like she wanted her old headlights back. She won't move until she's got them!'

From far away, a voice called, 'Coming! Ready or not!'

'It's them. They're looking for us now!' Lucy ran to the door of the garage and looked out. Nanny was heading for the house. The front door was opening. Maybe Tiny Jack was going to come out. Earlier Lucy had had an overwhelming desire to see what he looked like; now she had an even bigger desire *not* to see what he looked like. Her genius plan was this: she switched on her end of the baby monitor and spoke into it. 'Warmer. Getting warmer, Nanny.' She quickly turned it off.

Lucy had plugged the other end of the baby monitor into the socket behind the cupboard on the landing. Nanny now heard the voice coming from inside the house. Thinking that Lucy was in there she rushed inside to find her. Lucy ran back to help Jem.

In the corner of the room Jem spotted something covered with tarpaulin. He pulled the canvas off and smiled. The wheels – the speedy-looking wheels with their dazzling spokes and 'Zborowski' written on the hub, the wheels that Nanny had excavated in the desert.

'Lucy, help me move these. Ten minutes and we'll be out of here,' he said.

Lucy turned her end of the baby monitor on again and said, 'Warmer and warmer, Nanny,' into it, then hurried back to help Jem. But something was wrong. Very wrong. Jem was standing still, barely breathing, staring down at his wrist as though under some magic spell. Lucy followed his gaze. There, twitching on the back of Jem's hand, was a fat, hairy tarantula.

'This is the security system,' said Jem, trying not to move even his lips. 'Maybe it's not poisonous.'

'It's a Venezuelan flying tarantula. It's as poisonous as they come,' said Lucy. 'Stay very still and maybe it'll think that you're dead.'

'Why's it called that?' As he asked that, the tarantula seemed to screw itself up in a ball and then sprang on to his head. 'Can you knock it off maybe?'

As Lucy very gingerly lifted her hand to brush it away, something dark and twitchy shot up and landed on her shoulder. She froze. She could see another spider climbing out from among the tyres . . . Trying not to move her left side, she put her right hand on Little Harry's head and

pushed him away. Just in time. He fell over as another spider went arcing over his head.

There was a spluttering noise behind them. Then a rumble. Someone had turned on Chitty's engine. Smoke was pouring out of the exhaust.

'Football!' shouted Little Harry, kicking a spider into the air.

Who had started Chitty's engine? She must have started herself. The room was filling with deadly petrol fumes from Chitty's exhaust. Little Harry was struggling to breathe. Lucy wanted desperately to cough, but was scared that if she moved the spider would bite her. Dead.

'Stupid car,' she muttered.

Chitty's not stupid though, thought Jem. She's up to something. I just don't know what . . . He was desperate to cough, to breathe. His eyes were streaming, the inside of his nose was burning from the poisonous fumes. He heard something fall at his feet with a soft, pulpy *splat*. He looked down. The spider! If it was bad for the children to breathe in the fumes, it was even worse for the spiders. Another *splat*. The spider had fallen from Lucy's shoulder too. They were saved! Jem picked up Little Harry and put him in the van where there was still some fresh air. He tried to turn the engine off but Chitty was having none of it.

'Oh, Chitty, I can't change your wheels if I can't breathe. You have to stop. We have to get out of here right now.'

'Jem,' coughed Lucy, 'Jem . . .' She could barely speak.
'What?'

Even through the smoke he could see the fear and despair in her eyes.

'What's happened?'

'I forgot to turn the baby monitor off. Nanny and Tiny Jack . . . they must have heard everything. They know what we're up to.'

Suddenly the smoky room filled with light. Someone had opened the garage door, letting the light in and the smoke out. They could hear the someone coughing. They could see a giant wobbling shadow looming in the smoke.

'The wheels,' hissed Jem. 'Throw them in the back.'

Gasping for breath, they rolled the wheels over to Chitty and hurled them into the back of the van. Jem jumped into the driving seat. 'Chitty,' he said, 'I know you're a camper van, but I think you understand us. We can't fit the wheels right now but we have got them. I promise, we'll fit them as soon as we are . . .' The smoke had thinned now. He could see someone standing right in front of him. ' . . . as soon as we are safe.'

'Found you!' said the figure in front of the van. It was Nanny. She smiled and lifted her sunglasses. 'Tiny Jack is very, very upset. But I'm sure I can cheer him up.' She held out a hand. 'Give me the Lightning. I can't wait to see his smile when he sees it.'

Jem and Lucy wound the windows down and gulped in the fresh air. They had barely taken one lungful when Nanny was standing beside Lucy's door. Quickly Lucy wound up the window and made sure the door was locked.

'Put the car back and Nanny will make it all better,' said Nanny through the glass.

'There's one thing you don't know about our car,' yelled Jem. 'Chitty Chitty Bang Bang can fly!'

'What a lovely coincidence,' chirped Nanny.

'What does she mean?' said Jem. Then outside, beyond the door, he noticed something strange about the palm trees. They were thrashing around in an insane dance, their branches whipping about like mad hairdos, their trunks bending over as though an invisible hand was pressing down on them.

'What's that?'

'Helicopter!' yelled Little Harry.

He was right. A sharp-nosed blue-and-yellow helicopter, its tail raised high behind it like a scorpion's, shot into the sky in front of them, hovering there like a terrible hornet.

'There's something funny about that helicopter,' said Lucy. 'It's all kind of squarey on the edges.'

'It's made of Lego,' said Jem. 'That must be Tiny Jack . . .'

The helicopter came plunging down towards them, its rotor blades battering the air like raging swords.

Jem drove quickly forward, shooting right out of the garage, under the helicopter, heading for the edge of the deck.

Chitty went faster and faster towards the barrier. The

blades of Tiny Jack's evil helicopter spun in a blur. Chunks of Lego came thudding down on top of the van, exploding into cascades of blue and yellow bricks.

'Look out!' yelled Lucy. 'We're being blitzed with Lego bombs.'

Nothing could stop Chitty. She was powering towards the metal fence that was all that stood between them and the ocean.

'It's not me. It's Chitty,' shouted Jem. 'We have to trust Chitty. She'll save us. She'll fly us out of here.'

Lucy gripped her seat. They really were a long way up, and underneath them was the shark-infested ocean.

Jem's hands tightened on the steering wheel. In the rear-view mirror, he could see the helicopter right on his tail. It was getting so close he could make out the outlines of the individual bricks. Even as adrenalin flooded his veins, Jem found himself thinking, You have to admire Tiny Jack, building a Lego helicopter that can really fly.

Chitty smashed through the handrail and shot into the air.

There was a whistling noise and then an almighty splash and a jolt as the van hit the water in a blaze of foam and bubbles.

This time, Chitty Chitty Bang Bang had not taken off into the wild blue yonder.

She was sinking like a stone into the cold blue sea.

The sea into which Chitty Chitty Bang Bang was sinking was the Arabian Sea. It's famous for its clear waters, its turtles and tuna, and for its stunning coral reefs, which are thronged with brilliantly coloured clownfish, triggerfish, angelfish, lion fish, sea anemones, sea urchins and dugongs.

Jem and Lucy and Little Harry didn't see any of these things. All they saw was a storm of bubbles whirling past their windows as they plunged down, down, down towards the unlit, lifeless deep.

'I was so sure,' sighed Jem.

'And now we are so doomed,' said Lucy.

'At least we've got rid of Tiny Jack,' pointed out Jem.

As the van sank deeper and deeper into the ocean they peered into the gloom.

'Do you notice anything unusual about these bubbles?' Jem asked.

Chitty's windscreen was still covered in bubbles. It

was like being inside a huge Aero chocolate bar.

'The bubbles are not going upwards, they're going backwards. We are travelling forward. We're not sinking, we're sailing. Underwater.'

Lucy looked out of the window. On either side of Chitty Chitty Bang Bang – just where the wings had been – two great tanks of air had appeared. At the back, out of one of the exhausts, a large propeller was slowly, powerfully churning the water, sending the van forward.

Jem looked at Lucy. 'So,' he said, 'Chitty doesn't just fly. She's also a submarine.'

The water at this depth was utterly dark, like an ocean-sized version of Lucy's bedroom. Every now and then tiny glowing fish flickered past – like traffic on a faraway night-time motorway. Sometimes strange luminous plants drifted up to the split windscreen and hung there, like weird Christmas lights.

Then up ahead they saw a big single light moving quickly towards them. 'It looks like the headlight of an underwater motorbike,' said Jem.

'There's no such thing as a submarine motorbike,' said Lucy.

'There's no such thing as an underwater camper van,' said Jem, 'but here we are driving in one. For all we know, we're about to hit a massive submarine traffic jam.'

They weren't. Because it wasn't a headlight. It was an eye. Huge, unblinking, unmistakably an eye.

'That can't be real,' said Jem.

'Yes it can,' said Lucy. 'It is. It's the biggest eye in the world, the eye of a colossal squid. It's like a giant squid but much bigger and scarier. It's got hooks as well as suckers on its tentacles. It's unusual to find one this far north. It must be our unlucky day. Anyway, that's its eye. It looks like it's seen us. Like I said, unlucky.'

Chitty Chitty Bang Bang shuddered and shook as though she was afraid. But it wasn't fear. It was tentacles. The tentacles of the colossal squid can be forty feet long (which is why, even though its terrible eye was still a long way off, its vicious, hooked tentacles were already entwined around Chitty's front axle and her bumper). The colossal squid overcomes its enemies by squirting gallons of black ink at them (which is why Lucy and Jem and Little Harry felt as though darkest night had suddenly fallen). It attacks its prey with its beak (which is shaped like a parrot's but the size of a shovel).

The squid whacked Chitty's side with one huge, suckered tentacle and then another. Its hooks dragged them down into the deep. Even blinded by ink, the children knew they were going downwards. The air in the van turned really cold, and not just cold but strangely heavy and dense, as though something was squeezing it. Chitty shuddered as her bodywork was crushed and crumpled by the sheer weight of the water.

'Go away!' shouted Little Harry, and he thumped Chitty's horn.

'Don't do that!' said Lucy. 'We need to think.'

Jem reached past her and thumped the horn again.

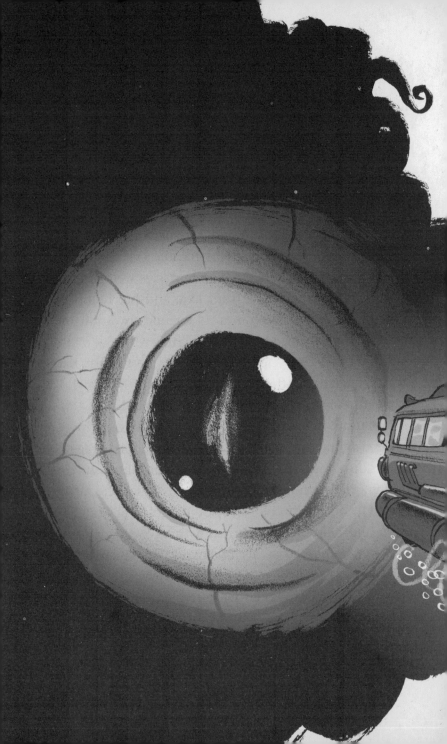

'I said, don't!' yelled Lucy.

Jem tooted the horn again.

'What are you doing?'

'Didn't you notice? Watch. I mean, listen. I mean, feel.' He pressed the horn once more. Longer. Harder. Keeping his hand on it. There. Lucy could feel it too. A shiver seemed to run through the whole of Chitty, a shiver that came from the tentacles.

'The sound goes right down the squid's tentacles,' said Jem. 'It tickles. The giant squid is ticklish!'

He pounded on the horn again. Again and again. Every time the squid shook and shivered until it just couldn't take it any more. Its tentacles curled up as though it was hugging itself. Chitty Chitty Bang Bang broke free.

They rose slowly through the water, passing from the dark of the depths into the golden green shallows where the coral grows and the colourful fish graze, and into the bright water near the surface where a shoal of quick silver fish swarmed around Chitty as though she might be something to eat.

When she finally broke the surface, the fish leaped from the water and flew over her as if waving goodbye. Lucy and Jem and Little Harry applauded in pure delight.

Suddenly a face appeared at the driver's window. For a terrifying moment they thought it was Tiny Jack or Nanny.

It was a man in a long green boat waving a big oar and using it to splash them, all the time shouting and waving his fist.

Lucy wound her window down so that she could hear him, and translated. 'He's speaking Malagasy,' she said. 'So I was right when I said we were heading to Madagascar. Malagasy's an interesting language. It's not related to any of the other languages in Africa, but it has a lot in common with languages from Borneo and the Philippines.'

'So you speak it then?'

'No. But he probably speaks French anyway. Most people in Madagascar do. *Excusez-moi, parlez-vous français?*'

The fisherman did speak French. He spoke a lot of it. Very quickly and loudly while waving his fist in the air.

'He's a fisherman,' said Lucy, 'who thought he'd caught something huge. Now he's disappointed that he'd just snagged his line on Chitty's bumper. Better not mention that he did have a colossal squid but that you tickled it away. He's really, really cross.'

The man had now dropped his oar into his boat and was clambering across on to Chitty, climbing in through the window.

'Apparently he gets seasick and now he wants a lift home. I think it's the least we can do.'

The man curled up on the back seat, occasionally groaning.

'Isn't being a fisherman a strange job for someone who gets seasick?' said Jem.

'I don't think he's in the mood to discuss his career choices,' said Lucy. 'His name is Fury, and I think he earned it.'

*

Soon trees appeared on the horizon and there were birds in the air that were not gulls. Then the beach appeared – a white beach in a narrow bay, with thickly wooded cliffs rising steeply behind it. Beyond that, delicate blue mountains. A cluster of square huts with pointy roofs was hidden among the trees. Although the huts were simple – small and made of tin and branches – each one had a satellite dish on the roof and a plasma screen TV on the porch. At one end of the beach was a much bigger hut that seemed to be a jigsaw of scrap. A man with a beard sat sunning himself under a sign that read 'Professor Tuk-Tuk's Miraculous Seaside Maritime Repair'.

'Exactly as I predicted,' said Lucy. 'We've hit the top of Madagascar. That mountain must be Maromokotro, the highest on the island.'

As Chitty ploughed through the surf and up on to the sand, dragging the green boat behind her, three children – a little boy, his big brother and a teenage girl – came running up to greet Mr Fury. He got out of the van and swung the toddler up in the air. He tickled him and put him on his shoulders, then he pointed to Chitty and snarled. Then his children looked at Chitty and they snarled too. Particularly the girl. She strode across, kicking up sand as she came. She pushed back her black hair and stared at Lucy with her black eyes, which were painted with very, very black eyeliner. 'My dad,' she said in perfect English, 'says you ruined his chances of catching a colossal squid today, and now all he has to show for a day at sea is this piece of junk.'

'We're sorry,' said Jem. 'And Chitty's not a piece of junk.'

'*Tsy ratsy kosa zany*,' repeated Lucy, in perfect Malagasy.

'That wasn't French,' said Jem.

'No, that was Malagasy.'

'You don't speak Malagasy.'

'I do now. Not well. Just enough to get by.'

Mr Fury's teenage daughter stared at Lucy. 'You speak Malagasy?'

Lucy stared back at the girl. 'So? You speak English.'

'I speak a lot of languages.' The girl looked Lucy in the eye.

'For instance? *Satria maninona?*' said Lucy in perfect Malagasy.

'French, German, Mandarin Chinese . . .' said the fierce girl.

'Cantonese, Italian, Spanish, Arabic, a bit of Japanese . . .' challenged Lucy.

'Japanese? Really? What are the verbs like?'

'Not as complicated as they look.'

'Cool,' said the girl, opening the door of the van. 'Come and teach me the proper use of the subjunctive, and maybe I'll let you live.'

When she had finished speaking, the girl's father said to her, *'Where did you learn to speak English?'*

'In my bedroom. What do you think I'm doing in there all day? My eyeliner?'

'You do always have perfect eyeliner.'

'*I study English,*' his daughter replied, '*and French, German and Mandarin Chinese.*'

'What was your dad saying?' Lucy asked as she strolled up the beach with the girl.

'Nothing much. He underestimates me.'

'Mine too,' said Lucy.

Little Harry toddled up the beach after them. Jem sat in the driver's seat, watching the others with a stab of loneliness.

The Tooting family was broken into pieces and the pieces were scattered just like the pieces of Chitty had been. The difference was that Chitty knew how to put herself back together, but Jem didn't know what to do.

The boy came over with a football and held it up as if to say, 'Want to play?' but Jem shook his head, then called Lucy out of the window. 'Let's get out of here! We need to find Mum and Dad.' He got out of the van and turned the crank handle impatiently. Once again Chitty wouldn't start.

'Come on,' growled Jem.

'Told you it was junk!' shouted the fierce girl. Jem ignored her and tried

again. Nothing happened. The girl called out something Jem didn't understand.

'She says you'll flood the engine,' shouted Lucy. 'Her name is Flora and she painted her bedroom black just like mine. Can you believe that?'

Jem didn't want to know. He just wanted his parents back. He dropped the crank on the sand and prowled away up the beach.

Lucy and Flora talked using words and phrases from every language they could think of. It was like a game of verbal snap. Flora told Lucy how in the old days you could catch fish and dig up turtle eggs just by rolling your trousers up, but now that the sea was getting dirtier fishing wasn't

what it used to be. People had to sail further and further from shore to catch the fish. Dad hated his job because he always got seasick and never caught anything. He really wanted to be in catering but as everyone cooked for themselves there was no call for that line of work.

The only man on the island who was really happy, she said, was Professor Tuk-Tuk. His philosophy was: 'There's no such thing as rubbish.' Whenever anything was washed up on the beach, he would take it apart and make it into something new. Nearly all the boats in the bay were made from bits of washed-up cars and white goods. 'That's why they all have such strange names,' said Flora. 'Like Allegro and Hoover and Capri. I like those names. But our boat has an unpronounceable name. Everyone says it's unlucky.'

'But you must be able to pronounce the name,' said Lucy. 'You can pronounce anything.'

'Of course I can,' said Flora. 'It's—'

'LUCY! COME QUICK! COME AND LOOK AT THIS!'

It was Jem. While he'd strolled up the beach, Mr Fury and his son had started walking around Chitty, looking under her sills and even opening her bonnet, trying to figure out what was wrong with her. It reminded Jem so much of himself and his own dad that he couldn't bear to watch, so instead he looked at Mr Fury's big green strangely shaped boat. Its body was like a huge metal canoe, but with four semicircular pieces missing – as though someone had taken a bite out of each corner. In the back were two plump couches with red leather upholstery. There was a big old steering wheel. The boat's name was written in curly steel letters along the front of the prow. It was written upside down. Jem had to turn his head sideways to read it.

Jem was still spelling it out for himself when Lucy started running towards him. He looked up in excitement and called to her, 'Lucy! Here! The name . . . !'

The name was, of course, Zborowski.

Jem looked back down the beach to where Mr Fury and his son were still inspecting Chitty Chitty Bang Bang and he knew at once that there was nothing wrong with her engine. Of course there wasn't. It worked eight fathoms under the sea and in the blistering heat of the desert. It wouldn't work here because Chitty didn't want it to. Chitty was going nowhere until she got her body back.

Flora thought Jem was just admiring the boat. 'Professor Tuk-Tuk made it,' she said, 'from parts of cars and trucks that were washed up on the beach.'

'I know,' said Jem. 'The hull is part of Chitty Chitty Bang Bang. Lucy, look – look at it upside down. It's the bodywork of a car – a car with a massive engine. This is Chitty's original body.'

Lucy bent over and put her head between her knees. 'Oh yes!' she said. 'It's obvious now. Wasn't she lovely? Kind of retro . . .'

'Wait,' said Flora. 'Are you saying you think our boat is yours?! We need our boat!'

'Yes, Jem, how would they make a living without

their boat? It would be a tragedy,' said Lucy.

'I love a tragedy,' said Flora. 'Except when it happens to me. You can't have the boat.'

'Chitty Chitty Bang Bang has flown us all over the world, looking for parts of herself. She's crossed seas and deserts and escaped from Tiny Jack and his nanny. She won't leave until she gets her body back . . .'

'So we'll be lost forever on a beautiful island, with some nice people and excellent seafood.' Lucy shrugged. 'Could be worse.' But the moment she said that she knew she didn't mean it.

'All that Chitty wants,' said Jem, 'is to be herself again.'

In the end, the solution was pancakes.

Mr Fury wanted a job in catering but he had nothing and nowhere to cook.

Jem had an idea. 'When we were in Cairo,' he said, 'people thought Chitty was a van selling pancakes. They queued for miles as soon as they smelt them cooking. I can show you how. You give us your boat, we give you the van. The perfect pancake van.'

'A van that sells pancakes?' said Mr Fury. 'That might just work.'

'Camper Van Pancakes,' said Baby Fury.

'Camper Van Pancakes.' Mr Fury rolled the words around in his mouth as if he was trying to taste them. 'The word today,' he said, 'is *that's the best idea I've heard in years.*'

'That's actually eight words,' said Jem, thinking sadly of Dad.

'In fact, ' said Lucy, 'in Malagasy the best idea I've heard in years – *hevitra tena faran'ny tsara reko hatramin'izay* – is actually six words – though it sounds like more.' Then she added, 'I miss Dad too.'

If you've ever been to Madagascar, you'll know that Jem's idea worked a treat. You can see Camper Van Pancakes vans in every town along the coast, and even in the central highlands, selling pancakes just like Mr Tooting used to make.

But what about the rest of the plan?

When Professor Fred Tuk-Tuk saw Chitty Chitty Bang Bang's bulging curly exhausts and barn-door radiator he stroked his beard and tilted his head. 'This,' he said, pointing at Chitty, 'belongs with this,' and he pointed to the Furys' boat. 'Please bring them both into Professor Tuk-Tuk's Miraculous Seaside Maritime Repair.'

They all helped wheel the camper van into Professor Tuk-Tuk's workshop. Then Professor Fred Tuk-Tuk closed the doors. For two days everyone along the beach could hear the sounds of hammering, soldering, welding and pummelling. At the end of two days, the professor opened the door a little and called to the children to come and help him polish the brasswork and smarten up the paintwork. For a whole day they polished and painted in there and everyone else sat on the sand, wondering when it would all end.

The doors of the garage finally opened and into the sun rolled Chitty Chitty Bang Bang's radiator – cleaned and polished and tall like a set of park gates. The minute they saw this, people started cheering. The cheering got louder when the front wheels rolled into view – their spokes flashing silver. And louder again as the wheels were followed by the bonnet – long and gleaming and majestic. When they saw the shining brass of her headlights, the flash of her mirrors, the snarling mouth of the big boa-constrictor horn and the rich red glow of her upholstery, the villagers went completely crazy. Professor Tuk-Tuk drove her out into the sunshine. Then she stopped.

The professor fiddled with the choke, gunned the clutch, but Chitty was going nowhere.

'Genius!' shouted Little Harry.

'Shhh,' said Lucy.

'Genius!' shouted Little Harry even louder, as Professor Tuk-Tuk bounced up and down in the driving seat muttering, 'Come on, you stupid car.'

Chitty is definitely not stupid, thought Jem. Neither is Little Harry. He followed his brother's gaze. Little Harry was staring at the wall of Professor Tuk-Tuk's garage. A wall that was made almost entirely of . . . of course . . . number plates. Chitty had no registration plate. There, in the midst of all the ordinary plates with their blocky numbers and letters were two very different from the rest – they were oval and the letters, written in a fine, flowing old-fashioned script – spelled 'GEN 11'. Jem ran over and took them down. Just at that moment, Chitty's headlights glowed, as though she was pleased. Of course that might only have been the sunlight glinting on her brass.

Jem smiled. 'Of course,' he said. 'Genius.' And he got the children into the car.

There has simply never been such a luxuriously comfortable car. The leather of the seats was soft as silk and the cushions were plump as pillows. The walnut of the dashboard, the brass and silver of her instruments shone like summer. There were elegant little recesses in the door specially made for maps and spectacles and bottles of eau-de-cologne, even one for cigars. (As they didn't have any cigars or bottles of eau-de-cologne Professor Tuk-Tuk had popped the jelly-baby phones in there.) In the glove compartment were five pairs of leather gloves and a thick leather-bound book.

'The logbook,' explained the professor. 'It contains the

entire history of this automobile. I found it on a shelf. I must have had it since the bodywork first washed up here, years ago. Everything is back the way it was.'

'She's the most beautiful car in the world,' said Jem.

'She's not a car,' said Mr Fury. 'She's a parade.'

It was true.

Jem leaned forward and pressed the shiny black self-starter button.

At first nothing happened. There was just the soft grinding from the starter motor. Jem and Lucy looked at each other. Wasn't she going to work after all?

Jem pulled out the silver choke to feed more petrol into the carburettor, and pressed the starter again. Out of the exhaust pipes there came just these four noises – very loud – CHITTY CHITTY BANG BANG!

There was a distinct pause after each noise, and it was like two big sneezes and two small coughs. There was silence.

Jem pressed the starter again. This time, after the first two CHITTY sneezes and the two soft BANGS, the BANGS ran on and into each other so as to make a delicious purring rumble, such as no one there had ever heard before from a machine.

Everyone sighed and then everyone applauded. Chitty Chitty Bang Bang, as if to show how much she enjoyed the applause, went, 'Chitty. Chitty. Bang! Bang!' once again.

Jem slipped Chitty into gear and as he drove carefully up the narrow road that wound through the cliffs and hills behind the village, children and young people followed waving and cheering.

'Wait, wait, wait . . .' called the Furys' son (now known as the Camper Van Pancake Boy). He ran after them and passed Jem the tiny silver aeroplane that had been hanging from the rear-view mirror.

'You nearly forgot this,' he said.

'Oh. Thanks,' said Jem.

'Goodbye,' shouted Flora, '*sayonara*, *au revoir*, *hasta luego*, *arrivederci* . . .' Her voice faded away as they climbed to the crossroads at the top of the cliff.

'I don't know which way to go,' said Jem.

'The last time we saw Mum and Dad,' said Lucy, 'was in Egypt. So I suggest we fly Chitty to Africa and then drive up through Mozambique.'

The newly restored dashboard had special buttons and handles for all Chitty's functions – the wings, the oxygen tanks, the electromagnetic front and rear bumpers. There were one or two that Jem didn't understand (what was the Chronojuster, for instance?) but it was good to know that you didn't have to drive off a cliff to get her to fly any more. They drove up high into the foothills of Maromokotro, where they found a nice wide meadow.

Jem engaged the wings and drove forward until they snagged on the air, caught and then wafted Chitty upwards and over the sea towards Africa.

Wherever they stopped for fuel and food as they drove towards Egypt they asked, 'Have you seen a couple – a man and wife – in a beautiful silver sports car with a bulletproof screen, headlights that pop up and an exhaust that can spray a smokescreen?'

'If we'd seen something like that, we would have remembered,' they said.

Then one day they drove through a village and out the other side and there were no more villages, just the desert. They flew north over a baking dust plain, floating from one thermal of hot air to the next.

They'd been travelling for days and nights, over swamps and forest and desert when Little Harry drummed his heels on the back of the seat. 'Mummy!' he shouted.

'We'll find her,' said Jem, 'don't you worry. One day we'll find her.'

'Actually the chances of that are fairly remote,' said Lucy. 'Just speaking realistically. We are very probably tragic orphans by now.'

'Mummy!' shouted Little Harry.

'What's that?' said Jem.

A strange dark shape was rocketing into the sky ahead of them. It was too fast and its flight was too vertical for a bird.

'Someone's shooting at us!' said Lucy. 'We're going to be dead tragic orphans. Or tragic dead orphans. Whichever sounds better.'

The shape seemed to stop in mid-air. Something like a huge flower blossomed from it. A parachute. They were closer to it now. It was a chair with a parachute attached to it. Someone was sitting in the chair.

'Mummy!' yelled Little Harry.

'Hello!' called the woman in the chair. 'If you could just . . . to the left . . . Jem . . . that's right.'

It was their mother!

Jem flew Chitty in a circle and Mum carefully steered her parachute and landed behind the front seats. The parachute descended gently on to their heads. It covered the whole car. Suddenly blinded, Jem lost control and Chitty went into a terrifying dive.

'We're all going to die!' came Lucy's muffled voice from under the swathes of parachute silk. 'Reunited and then dashed to our doom!'

Luckily the slipstream caught the parachute and blew it away. It flapped and flopped across the desert like a crazy ghost. When it was gone they could see Mum sitting there with Little Harry in her arms.

'We've been looking for you everywhere,' she said. 'Every village we went to, the people had seen you, so we followed your trail out here into the desert and then Dad looked up and spotted you in the sky. At first we thought you were an unusually large vulture, but then as we got closer we saw you were a car. We only know one flying car, so Dad suggested I get into the ejector seat, and here I am. Chitty's changed a bit. I see she's had a makeover.'

'Where is Dad?'

'If you look over to your left you'll see some armoured cars and soldiers and so on. That's the Aston Martin in the middle. It's completely surrounded.'

'Errm, why are the soldiers pointing their guns at Dad?'

'You tell me. Our car seems to have an awful lot of enemies because, honestly, everywhere we've been people have shot at us, chased us on motorbikes, set traps for us. We've got surprisingly good at car chases actually. This looks more serious though. I keep trying to persuade your father to trade in the car for a less conspicuous model. But he just loves that Aston. We'd better go and rescue him, I suppose.'

This wasn't as hard as it sounds, even though by the time they got to Dad a tank was rumbling up the dune towards him. Jem landed Chitty right in its path. The moment he did so, the soldiers lowered their guns. Some of them started clapping. They all wanted to have their photograph taken with Chitty. They apologized to Dad for nearly shooting him and he said that was quite all right and told them they could keep the Aston. Though he did have his photograph taken with it before the soldiers drove it away.

'You do look after us, Chitty,' said Mum.

'Yes,' said Dad. 'Where is Chitty?'

'This is Chitty,' said Mum, patting the car's bonnet appreciatively.

'How can this be Chitty? Chitty is a twenty-three-window Samba Bus beautifully restored by me and my son. This car is . . . I don't know what it is.'

'Dad! Shush!' warned Lucy. 'Chitty does have feelings, you know.'

'Yes, but that's not Chitty. Chitty is a camper van.'

'The thing is, Dad,' said Jem, 'I don't think Chitty is a camper van. I think Chitty is . . . Chitty. She's got a mind of her own. All the time we thought we were driving her, she was really driving us. She's been searching the world for all her missing components. She took us to the Eiffel Tower for her lights. Cairo for her wheels. And the bodywork – she found it in Madagascar. She's been putting herself back together.'

Dad crouched down and peered under the radiator. 'Well if she's putting herself back together, she's not doing a very good job. Who fitted this bodywork on to the chassis?'

'Professor Tuk-Tuk,' said Jem. 'The miraculous car restorer.'

'It's miraculous that it's all stayed together. Look at this. It's not lined up properly. And the tracking is all over the place. We'd better get home as soon as we can so you and I can finish the job properly.'

'Seemed like she was running quite nicely to me,' said Lucy. 'We did fly over the Arabian S– Ow!'

Mum had stepped on Lucy's toe. 'Quite right, Dad,' she said. 'Chitty definitely needs your help to get her back into shape.'

'My help, and Jem's,' said Dad, climbing into the driver's seat. 'The word today is *teamwork*.'

'Jem,' said Lucy quietly, as Jem sat down next to her, 'did you ever wonder how the headlights of a car that crashed in Dover ended up on top of the Eiffel Tower?'

'Or how the bodywork of a car that lost its wheels in Egypt ended up in Madagascar?' replied Jem.

'Or why anyone should take such a beautiful car and break it into pieces?'

'Or why, when they had, they'd go to so much trouble to spread the pieces all over the world?'

Chitty Chitty Bang Bang wasn't just a car. She was a mechanical mystery.

So the Tootings headed for home – across the Mediterranean and over the Pyrenees, north through France, doing a lap of the Eiffel Tower for old times' sake, sharing stories of their adventures.

Jem sat in the back with Lucy and Little Harry. He didn't want to drive Chitty any more. It was fun to drive, but to be in the back of your car while your parents were chatting and laughing up front, that was really special. Especially if the car happened to be floating through a starry night sky high above Paris.

'The car was built by Count Zborowski,' he said, leafing through the log book. 'And then a family owned it after that. The Pott family. They made a whole list of alterations. They're all in here. They must be the ones who put in the wings and the oxygen tanks and so on. It doesn't say where they went but there are lots of tickets and postcards. Argentina, Brazil, the North Pole . . .' As Jem read the names, Chitty's engine purred as if she was enjoying these reminders of travels long past. 'And here are all the technical specifications – horsepower, tyre pressure and . . . oh.'

'What?'

'It says here the engine came from a Sopwith-Lightning. What's that?'

'It sounds like an old-fashioned plane. That would make sense. It's an aircraft engine.'

'When you say an old-fashioned plane, do you mean one with two sets of wings and a big propeller? A plane like this . . .'

He took the little silver plane out of his pocket and held it up so that his dad could see it in the rear-view mirror.

'Yes. Something like that.'

'So this is it,' said Jem. 'I've had it all along, the Zborowski Lightning.'

'How lovely,' said Mum. 'Chitty's missing mascot.'

'It must be more than a mascot,' Jem replied. 'Nanny was prepared to feed us to the fish for it.'

As dawn was breaking they landed near the campsite on top of the white cliffs of Dover. They had decided to drive home, along roads, like normal people. It would feel more like a proper homecoming that way.

They stopped at a service station and all had a full English breakfast. Dad leaned back in his chair and looked at his family and he said, 'You know, I could live like this.'

As they were getting back into the car, Jem took out the silver aeroplane again and slotted it into the little hole in the top of the radiator cap. It fitted perfectly.

'The word today,' said Dad, 'is *finishing touch, cherry on the cake, grande finale.*'

'That's actually eight words,' said Lucy.

'It does look fine,' said Mum.

It looked even finer when they started to move, because the tiny propellors went round and round in the breeze. And Chitty's engine hummed as softly and smoothly as a distant aeroplane. You could tell she was glad to have her ornament back. 'Who would have thought,' said Dad, 'that a car would be so impressed by a toy aeroplane.'

'BANG BANG,' went Chitty's exhaust. She clearly took a dim view of people calling her silver plane a toy. But before the argument could go any further the car stopped. And so did all the cars around it. And behind it. And in front of it. Motorists raged and banged on their horns.

'Ah,' sighed Dad contentedly, 'congestion on the eastbound carriageway of the M25. Now I feel like I'm really home.'

Out of the blue came a voice. 'ANSWER THE PHONE!' Everyone jumped. 'ANSWER THE PHONE! WHY IS EVERYONE IGNORING ME?' It was the voice of Tiny Jack. Everyone looked around.

'It's all right,' said Jem. 'It's just the phone. That's his ringtone. Look . . .' The lemon jelly-baby phone was glowing prettily in its special little eau-de-cologne-bottle slot in Chitty's door.

'I'll answer it,' said Dad. 'I owe him an apology really. We got bullet holes in his Aston Martin. And then we gave it away.'

'No!' yelled Lucy and Jem. 'Don't touch it!'

'The children are right. You mustn't use the phone while you're driving. I'll get it.'

'ANSWER ME!'

'NO!' said Lucy. 'Please don't.'

As Mum reached for the phone, Chitty lurched into reverse. Mum was thrown back into her seat. The phone tumbled to the floor. Suddenly the big shiny handle of Chitty's Chronojuster clunked to the bottom of its slot. Before they knew it, the car was speeding backwards down the middle lane.

'Dad! You can't do this!' yelled Jem. 'You're driving backwards down the motorway . . .'

Lucy couldn't bear to look. Little Harry put his fingers in his ears. Jem stared in horrified fascination at the cars behind them rushing towards them. Except they weren't rushing towards them. They seemed to be going backwards too. It wasn't a motorway any more, just an ordinary road.

We seem to have taken the exit without noticing . . .' said Dad, as they reversed into a quiet road with thatched cottages on either side. They went backwards past a field of horses, a pond full of ducks, a hedgerow decked with May blossom. 'Basildon town centre,' said Dad, 'is a lot greener than I remember.'

They backed down a narrow country lane, twisting

and turning through clumps of huge mossy trees. 'I must say,' observed Dad, 'the council have really let the roads go these last few weeks.'

'Yes,' replied Mum. 'I'm sure this corner was where World of Leather was.'

'And the SuperBowl Ten Pin Bowling Centre was just there,' said Jem. 'Now it's just trees.'

'That's good,' said Dad. 'Trees are good.'

But he couldn't help but notice that the lane no longer had tarmac and road signs. It was just a track, a white dusty track cut into the chalk. The trees too were surprisingly tall. They were thicker. The air was damp

and hot. The undergrowth was thick and steamy. So thick and steamy that Chitty had to stop to catch her breath (the engine was air-cooled).

'Dinosaurs!' shouted Little Harry.

'Yes, yes, when we get home we'll find your dinosaur,' said Mum. 'Now shush while I check the map. We seem to be lost.'

But Jem knew that you should never tell Little Harry to be quiet. Never ignore what he was saying. If Little Harry said dinosaurs, then that strange, heavy thumping that seemed to be coming nearer and nearer through the trees . . . that splintering of wood and crunching of rocks . . . that hideous, mucousy roar that almost deafened you . . .

'I know this sounds strange,' said Mum, pointing nervously off to the left, 'but isn't that . . . ?'

'Dinosaurs!' yelled Little Harry.

'Tyrannosaurus rex, to be precise,' said Lucy, 'from the Latin for "king of the terrible lizards".'

'The word today,' said Dad, 'would seem to be *Jurassic*.'

'Not to be picky,' observed Lucy as the giant beast came crashing towards them through the trees, 'but I think you'll find that the word today is actually *Eretaceous*.'

'Dinosaurs!'

'I think Chitty just engaged her Chronojuster,' said Jem, leafing quickly through the logbook and manual. 'It says here, "Do not engage the Chronojuster unless –"' he looked up – '"time travel is required . . ."'

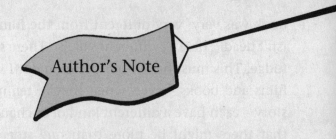

The very first proper film I ever saw in the cinema was *Chitty Chitty Bang Bang*. I remember a lot of things about that day – for instance the big helping of cherry lips I got from Woolworth's Pick'n'Mix beforehand. But the thing I remember most is the moment when Chitty drives off the edge of the cliff with the family on board. The whole cinema howled with fear and frustration because the picture froze and the word 'Intermission' blazed across the screen. I sat through the next ten minutes not even looking at the sweets I'd so carefully picked and mixed, just waiting for the movie to start up again. That was the day I discovered that a story could be even better than cherry lips!

Even now, whenever I come across a really heart-stopping moment in a script or a story, I think of it as a 'Chitty falls off the cliff' moment.

Because I didn't want the film to be over, I followed the car's smoky trail to the library and found Ian Fleming's book *Chitty Chitty Bang Bang – The Magical Car*, which he'd written for his son, Caspar, in 1964. I thought that if I read it I would see the whole movie again inside my head. I was surprised to find that the book was very, very different from the film. The mum isn't dead. There's a different villain. There's a recipe for fudge! This must have been the moment I learned that films and books – even when they're telling the same story – each have a different kind of enchantment. And that there might be more than one story – or more than a hundred – ways to tell the same story. As the old Tuscan proverb says: 'The tale is not beautiful if nothing is added.'

It felt strange at first writing a new instalment of someone else's story. But in the end isn't that what we always do when we tell stories – take something old and give it something of ourselves in the hope that it will fly once more?

So I'd like to thank Lucy Fleming, Kate Grimond and Robert Laycock for lending me their vintage car and letting me play with it (for longer than I said I would); Sarah Dudman – my incomparable editor – for finding and tuning the engine; Talya Baker for keeping track of all the thousands of screws and washers that hold the machine together. Thanks too to Solofo Eric Rakotoarisoa for the lesson in Malagasy and to George Sarkis for the lesson in Egyptian Arabic. Also to James Clay for unparalleled camper-van knowledge.

Above all, as ever, I have to thank my wife Denise, who is forever driving us off the edges of cliffs while convincing us that we can fly.

Frank Cottrell Boyce's books are enjoyed around the world by readers of all ages. They have won or been shortlisted for every major UK award. His first novel, *Millions*, was made into a feature film. His second, *Framed*, was adapted for BBC television. His third book, *Cosmic*, is currently being developed for cinema.

Frank is also a successful screenwriter and is helping to devise the Opening Ceremony for the London 2012 Olympic Games.

Joe Berger is a children's author, illustrator and cartoonist. In 2011 he was a winner of Booktrust's Best New Illustrators Award. He makes prize-winning animated short films and is co-creator of the food cartoon in the *Guardian* magazine each Saturday. Joe was the official illustrator for World Book Day 2010.